Letters for Annie:
Memories from World War II

The Untold Story of the Lombardo Family Letters

By Joseph McGee

ENJOY!

John F Conrad

Abstract Publications
Bristol, CT 06010
Web: **http://abstractpublications.us**

Cover Design By: Joseph McGee
Concept & Letters Provided By: John Lombardo

Requests to the author can be made by contacting Abstract Publications at **books@abstractpublications.us**

ISBN-13: 978-1981945443
First Edition, January 2019

www.lettersforannie.com

HISTORICAL FICTION

Main Characters

Based on Letters
(PFC) Pat Lombardo, US Army
(S4C) John Lombardo, US Navy
(MR1) Tony Lombardo, US Navy
(MM/Radio) Vic Lombardo, US Navy
(Lt. Commander) "Junior" US Navy

Based on Real Events
(LT/CAPTAIN) Leon Grabowsky, US Navy

Present
Annie Connerton (Original Recipient of the letters)
John Lombardo (Present keeper of the letters)
Tony Lombardo (2007)

Foreword by John Lombardo

My name is John Lombardo. This book is about letters that were sent to my Aunt Annie from her four brothers while they were away during the war; you know the big one, World War II. Her four brothers include my dad Vic, and my Uncles John, Pat, and Tony. Annie was a sweet woman, with a big heart, so it doesn't surprise me that she kept these letters all those years.

Here is how the letters ended up in my hands. My Aunt Annie had passed away in 2007. One year later, while at a birthday party for my Uncle Tony who was turning 80 years old, my cousin Richard hands a box to me that his dad, Tony had found in my Aunt Annie's condo after she had passed. He simply says to me, "here take this, I'm sure you'll know what to do with it".

We didn't discuss the box again the rest of that day. At the time the only thing that I knew was they were letters that my aunt had received and saved from her brothers, including my dad, Vic, during the war. I took the box and placed it in my office at home, and didn't look through it for at least a year. When I sat down to look through the box, I had no real expectations regarding the contents and the impact they would have on me.

The first thing that moved me was the fact that they were all handwritten in my dad's, Vic, and my uncles, John, Pat, and Tony's handwritten styles.

I began to go through the letters sorting them into piles of each loving brother's thoughts captured on paper during what I can only imagine as a time of extreme stress in the world, including for the Lombardo family. Although my dad and I never spent time discussing the war, and what he witnessed, I do know that, even though his parents were immigrants from Sicily, they were proud that their sons where fighting for freedom for their newly adopted country, America.

As I slowly sorted the letters into piles from each of my uncles and my dad, I began to think that there is a story here that should be shared. I knew that I would never have the discipline to write a book, so I started a search for someone who would find this discovery of letters a great foundation for a book. My thoughts were, what a great way to honor my dad, and his brothers, as well as my beautiful Aunt Annie. I quickly found that not everyone who I discussed the possibility of a novel was as interested as me. Almost every author I talked to said the same thing, this is your family story, and you should write the book. Knowing that I'm anything but an author, I continued my search. There was times when I thought that my cousin Richard was wrong when he said as he handed me the box, "here take this, I'm sure you'll know what to do with it". It took a long time to find an author who showed the same interest as me, but my persistence paid off. I called Joe McGee, someone I had worked with at a large insurance company, who I had recently published to books and might find this project of interest. He showed the same interest as me!

This book although not non-fiction is still based on many facts and the letters found after my aunt had passed. I often wonder why she had kept the letters, and why my cousin had handed them to me back in 2007. Did my aunt hope that someday my dad and uncles would be honored through the written word in a book? Maybe she simply couldn't throw them away, or maybe she had hoped that someday someone would recognize that there is a story here and it needed to be shared. We will never know.

www.lettersforannie.com

Who is Annie?

During World War II – Annie received hundreds of War Letters from her brothers who served in the military. This story will showcase the stories of the Lombardo Family Letters with Annie telling their story. This is the untold story of the Lombardo Family letters. What did family members say about Annie?

From: Cousin Santo

When I think of Auntie Annie I don't have a lot of warm fuzzy memories. I recall a soft-spoken but strong woman who loved her family but interestingly didn't have the sense of humor that the Lombardo men had. I recall when she was bedridden towards the end of her life my father was using her Cadillac and got into some kind of fender bender and he was very nervous about her finding out that he wrecked her car even though she would never drive again. She was always nice to my kids on the few times we visited always seemed to have candy for them.

From: Lynn Lombardo Mejias | Pat's Youngest Daughter

My Aunt Annie was one of a kind, a soft-spoken lady who I have never witnessed her ever being in a bad mood. Although she never had children, Aunt Annie kept in touch with all of her nieces and nephews making each of them feel special. From Sunday visits when I was a child to talking to her on the phone the memory was always pleasant.

As time went on and I had my own family she enjoyed coming over to visit us and often brought Rice Krispie treats to my children that she had made. The later years of her life I would drive my Father Pat to her house to play cards with her, my Uncle Jim and my Aunt Marilyn. She looked forward to this and I did as well.

I remember that great cup of perked coffee that she made on the stove along with the cookies she would serve afterward. She witnessed many family losses along the way and that affected her life dearly.

Aunt Annie loved her entire family and she changed all of our lives with her unselfish act of kindness leaving all her nieces and nephews with a special gift when she passed. I would like this opportunity to say thank you to my Aunt Annie for her generosity and the love she showed me throughout my life.

From: Lane Lombardo

I suppose I was a lucky girl growing up. My parents chose Anne and Jim Connerton to be my God Parents. As far back as I can remember I adored and looked up to Aunt Annie as some kind of soft-spoken Princess who could make anything possible and anything wrong, right. She was sweet and kind and a great listener. She was a symbol of success to me-worked (successfully) in a man's world, dressed impeccably all the time, never raised her voice to anyone, always lived in a well-appointed and maintained home, was the hostess who loved having family around and would always have a tin can of candies or cookies for the children and a pot of coffee on the stove and a pastry for the adults

She coddled and adored her kid brothers but could still throw down with them while playing hours and hours of cribbage or poker. Every one of her brothers tried jokes or outwit each other and she would laugh and shake her head in playful approval.

She knew I was interested in a career in nursing and she always encouraged me to follow that dream. Even when my Dad was adamant about not letting me attend college outside of Connecticut, it was Aunt Annie that convinced him to let me go to Vermont to study. She very proudly attended my graduation and continued to remind me about the purpose of hard work and giving back to others. I always wanted to be just like her-she was elegant, kind, intelligent and caring.

Aunt Annie was very frugal in everyday life and never purchased what she didn't need and was a true seeker of a bargain. She taught me to clip newspaper coupons and how to keep them organized so you had them when you needed them!

She never had children and one time told me that she and Uncle Jim regretted that, but she loved her nieces, nephews and the neighbor's children. She was an avid writer of letters. Even after I moved away to California, she and I would correspond regularly through letters. Her words seemed to flow and never lacked information to share with me or to keep me up to date on the family. I struggled with things to share thinking that she was such a great storyteller and my adventures would pale.

She was the voice of reason when my parents were making tough decisions with me or with family and simply always knew what to do, it seemed.

www.lettersforannie.com

As years went by my visits back home from California to Connecticut became more out of necessity when someone was ill or had passed away. I began to see the perfectly put together Aunt Annie wave a bit but she stilled maintained the figure of the Lombardo family Matriarch, a position in the family that we all gave her years ago. She was truly a lovely lady.

Table of Contents

Chapter 1: The Phone Call

May 23, 2007
Hartford, Connecticut

I received a frantic phone call from Annie who wanted more closure on the family war letters that I had in my possession. Annie resides in a hospice facility in Connecticut and for the past month is undergoing treatment and visited by family regularly as she doesn't have much time to live. John was surprised to hear such urgency in Annie's voice as this was outside Annie's demeanor. Annie had always remained calm and soft-spoken. This warranted John's immediate attention and knew something may have turned for the worst.

[Phone ringing]

John picked up the phone and realized after strong breathing and fast-paced speech it was Annie who was on the other line.

John with a worry in his voice said, "Annie. Take a deep breath and calm down. I can't understand you. Is everything ok?"

Annie replied, "John – something amazing happened last night. I had just watched the movie – Letters from Iwo Jima and it brought back memories from the war. Don't ask any questions. You need to do me a favor – ok?"

John said, "Ok – I'm listening…"

Annie continued with a worried voice and said, "You must come to me right now. Drop what you're doing. You still have the family war letters, correct?"

John said, "Sure do."

Annie said, "Call Tony and tell him to come with you. Bring the box of letters and I'll explain everything – you must hurry."

John said, "We'll be there within the hour."

[Phone disconnects]

Just a month prior Annie had provided me the box of letters for safekeeping and for the family to remember our roots. Call it luck of fate – for the letters to still be in pristine condition. I had a little scare with the letters after obtaining them. I had a flood and luckily enough the box of letters was placed on a top shelf high in the closet. If they were placed on the floor all of our memories would have been lost. If this happened – I would not know how to break the news to Annie. I knew that the purpose of these letters might warrant a book one day.

[Picks up the phone and calls Tony]

Tony answered the phone and said, "Hello..."

John replied, "Tony its John – How are you?"

Tony said, "John it's good to hear from you."

John said, "I received a frantic call today. Its Annie she's asking for both us to come down today and see her. I think this could be her last days here with us. Can you meet me down at the hospice within the hour?"

Tony said, "Oh gosh. Yes – I will be right over. See you soon."

John said, "See you soon."

[Phone hangs up]

I was very concerned about Annie's health and was not sure what the importance of the letters was at that moment. I had restrained myself from calling the main number at the hospice to confirm with the facility if anything might be different with Annie. I decided instead to grab the box of letters and hurry over to the hospice to get closure on the connection with the letters.

As I arrived on location many things popped into my mind that really concerned me. Was Annie getting Dementia? Would she even remember she called me? Or perhaps was this an attempt to get more closure and purpose in life as her dying wish?

I waited outside for Tony to arrive as I wanted to go inside as a group. A few moments later Tony had arrived and dropped off by a local Taxi service. He is 79 years old and not as mobile as he would like to be.

John saw Tony get dropped off as Tony was walking towards him with his cane; John had said, "Tony. I'm so glad to see you. Thanks for coming down. Are you ready to go inside? Do you need any help?"

Tony said, "John – I'm fine. Let's go inside."

[They proceeded to enter the hospice building]

As they turned the corner to enter Annie's room – we found her in a rocking chair in front of a window with her back faced towards me. The room was dark and I could feel a cold chill in the air. In that moment the lights started to flicker and dim as I slowly approached Annie in her chair.

John said, "Annie. Are you ok?" with much concern in his voice. Again and again he said, "Annie…my dear Annie. What's wrong," warranted no response after several attempts from John.

John looked at Tony as they progressed into the room.

[John was shaking his head and looked worried]

Tony said, "Sis it's me Tony – I'm here doll. Can you turn around to see us?"

[Again no response or movement had occurred]

Annie's room was on the third floor and offered a bay window with the curtains wide open overlooking a scenic view into the woods.

Suddenly as John approached within just footsteps of Annie with Tony a few steps behind – the weather turned for the worse. The flashes of lightning and dimming lights were quite unusual since the weather seemed fine on the way down to the facility.

As John reached the back of the rocking chair the power in the room went off forcing the emergency floodlights to kick on. Before John could turn his head to check on Annie he was drawn by a distant glow outside the window coming over the tree line.

John had noticed something forming and moving towards the window.

John said to Tony, "What is that?"

Tony said, "I'm not sure but it's getting closer to us."

[They both were focused on this object together]

It appeared to be a small cloud which was immediately taking shape into a bigger cloud with a white glow reflecting from the object.

John and Tony had wondered what was occurring and at that moment was so glued into this object he had forgotten about Annie and full attention on the object. As the object came closer and within about 10 feet from the window the object had morphed into three separate cloud shapes and dissipated as they hit the window. Not even a thud or a smack of water was seen on the window. Absolutely nothing was heard or seen.

Within 15 seconds the room became even colder. We're talking winter jacket weather.

Suddenly two objects that resembled fog at first started to morph into some human form unfolding in front of me. A faint voice is saying something, but I cannot make anything out nor can I see what these objects are transforming into.

As this was unfolding, I had glanced over at Annie and noticed her eyes were closed and she was not moving. My heart dropped to the floor and beyond the floor. In front of her at her feet was the DVD- Letters from Iwo Jima that she had mentioned during her phone call.

"She's gone! My poor Annie is gone", John said while drawing a bath of tears. At that moment, Tony had broken down and started to rubbing Annie's hand and was in a state of shock.

As this sadness had been realized the faint voice and objects are fully visible and heard.

"Hello, John and Tony! It's Vic and Pat," one voice had spoken.

I had looked up and my mouth fell to the ground. It was Vic, and Pat dressed in their armed forces outfits from the 1940s appearing in a ghost form.

"Holy Shit – its Vic and Pat – You're here and in your prime. Where is Uncle John, had said."

Pat said, "Are you kidding me. You know John is never on time for anything."

John said, "This is bringing back so many memories and stories that I have heard from the past through Annie and the letters."

Tony said, "Guys. You're here with us but what are you doing here?"

Vic said, "We have been watching over Annie for quite some time. All of us have. We had heard the phone call she made to you. We didn't want you or Annie not to have her closure as her dying wish. Annie is close by in the afterlife – we are here as Angels to take you to her."

At that moment it was John who had appeared late to arrive much like his time in the living world before he passed away.

John said, "Wow – guys you are all here and you look great and haven't changed one bit!! When I can see Annie – I said.

Vic said, "We're going to take you through – *The Sphere of the Holy Gate.*"

I had replied – The sphere of the what?

Vic said, "You see Annie just passed away not even ten minutes ago and we were waiting for her in – *The Sphere of the Holy Gate.* Think of it as an airport security checkpoint. It's the gate before you reach heaven. Annie is here now waiting for us. John and Tony, are you ready to see her?"

John said, "Yes – please I need to see her. My heart is shattered by seeing her like this now in this room. I just spoke to her about an hour ago."

Tony said, "Yes – but being I'm older will I be able to travel to this sphere – and arrive safely?

Vic said, "Tony we can bring you safely – Yes. Before we go thought we must plan accordingly."

John said, "What do you mean – plane accordingly?"

Pat said, "Yes Vic is right. It's like we can get on a Greyhound bus together. It needs to be planned – for your human body?"

John said, "What's going to happen to my human body."

Vic said, "John – Have you ever heard stories of ones who died and may have said – they have experienced well let's say an out of body experience?"

John said, "Yes. If I recall, I heard a story when someone described how their soul leaves the body and they are witnessing their human body. Perhaps they aren't dead and maybe come back to life – later on, to tell such a story."

Vic said, "Precisely [with much exhilaration in his voice."

John said, "I see what we mean. We can't leave the hospice to find our bodies here. I and Tony would have to come back and have to track every morgue in Connecticut for our bodies. But wait a minute…Guys! How many times have you actually done this before [worried voice]?"

Uncle John said, "I know I'm late for everything but I don't think we as a group have ever done this. Have we – guys?"

[Shouting in tune with each other's voice] NO – all the guys said.

Vic said, "Don't worry John you have to trust us. This is for Annie – we need to fulfill our wish. She's waiting for us. We must go now."

John said with a deep breath, "Ok – I trust you guys but I can't leave my body in this room."

We can't do it here. There is an old Oak Tree behind this building through the forest. Nobody should bother me here. I'll meet you over. Before I do go – should I tell someone about Annie? If I leave and not tell someone what if I'm pinched for murder?"

Tony said, "If we do tell someone it's going to lead into paperwork and how you would just storm out – like you dropped change in your pocket and it meant nothing?"

John said, "Tony and guys - I see your point. I have an idea though. It's almost 8:30 pm and visitor hours are almost over. I'm going to tell the nurse Annie is tired and is sleeping and not to be disturbed. This should give us some time to be with Annie. Meet me and Tony near the Oak Tree in 5 minutes down back."

[I made my way over downstairs and told the front desk nurse about Annie sleeping – and slipped outside]

John and Tony had arrived in front of the old Oak tree outside the hospice. They saw the same glow come towards him – it was the boys. This time all of us including John were together. They appeared in front of John once again.

John said, "Hey Uncle John – Are you sick?"

Uncle John said, "What do you mean- do I look green?"

John said with much sarcasm, "No – you're never on time for anything. Congratulations."

Vic said, "Ok John it's time. Close your eyes for me."

[Vic had touched me and it felt like a shot you would get at the hospital with a needle. Was just a pinch]

As I opened my eyes – I was in shock in what I saw…

Chapter 2:
The Sphere of the Holy Gate
May 23, 2007
The Holding Pattern for Heaven

The skies were like crystal blue water you would only see on a tropical island. Beneath my feet were slow moving clouds and endless and endless amounts of clouds with no bottom or depth to be seen beneath us. Just ahead – I saw a metal gold gate with the same phrase Vic had mentioned to me earlier. It said, "Welcome to The Sphere of the Holy Gate. To the right of me was Tony with the same look of excitement that I had."

As I and the boys had approached closer to the gates main entrance I felt something reach down into my chest and pump my heart. I felt alive again. Why do I feel better – I wondered?

Coming through the gate was a young woman dressed in a red ball gown from the 1940s. She had a pearl necklace on and was waving to me. As I squinted my eyes – It resembled a younger Annie. Is it really Annie?

She came closer and said, "John and Tony – you made it. Oh, thank god…"

John said, "Annie look at you. You look happy and full of so much energy. Look who I have behind me. Vic, Pat, and John are also here with us."

Annie said, "Smashing. Everyone is here. You have the letters as well – I cannot wait to read the letters. Not just read the letters but Tony, Pat, John, and Vic can now really tell their stories without a sensor editing or not allowing more details to be heard. I'm so happy right now."

Annie said, "Well. All of this started a few hours ago but seems like an eternity ago."

Annie said, "John. Yesterday the local hospice was playing the movie Letters from Iwo Jima that just came out on DVD. Have you seen it?"

Before I could answer her eagerness continued with her story…

Annie began to tell her story from reflections of watching the DVD. Annie said, "John in this movie the condition of the soldiers and state of mind started giving me flashbacks – you know from Vic, Tony, Pat, and John. It's like I was watching the movie through their eyes and then remembered all the war letters that they had sent me over the years. One scene in the movie struck a chord with me and knew I must share these memories with you know John. The Japanese had made man-made caves and as they were being attacked by the US whether from the sea or air or on land – the soldiers barely had time to read letters and possibly write the last letters of their life's. Most never fought in a real life combat situation and quite frankly were scared. I wondered the conditions of my brothers and where they were or what they saw before writing me these thoughtful letters. Can you imagine? As civilians, we forget that one would think the most immediate concern would be from the enemy. But John…It's more than just the enemy you see."

Annie continued to discuss what was important and overlooked in war. Annie said, "We think about the simplest things we overlook when thinking of war.

When we think of war; we think that's the most immediate threat at that moment – but it's not you see."

This movie opened my eyes. Think about the before and preparations of War. What the soldiers are enduring mentally and physically while training or while in combat. These conditions are often-overlooked and could bring a huge strain in the ability to carry out duties. I wondered what impact these conditions played a part during the war for Vic, Tony, Pat, and John.

I just passed away probably moments before you arrived. I was just so anxious to share memories with you – John.

Before we open the box of letters – I wanted to tell you a quick story to remind you of the humorous side of the Lombardo's. Tony can fill in any of the blanks in case I told the story wrong since he is in fact with us now. Did I ever tell you the story in the early 80's about the post office show off by Pat Lombardo?

John said, "No – I don't think so..."

Annie said, "Well, as you know most were very focused on their jobs after the war for the US Postal Service. Tony had just received the US Postal Office ELT Award recognition by his supervisor which recognizes superior individual contribution or achievement deserving of system-wide recognition. Tony had streamlined many processed which allowed productivity in his department to increase resulting in more time to do other tasks that normally would bleed into the other day. The Postmaster had called a dinner party in celebration of his achievement. This was a formal gathering with friends and family in attendance to honor Tony. I didn't tell you this story?"

John said, "No but given our family's blend of serious humor I'm dying to hear more."

Annie said, "Well you're going to love this. You see Pat shows up to the event in a black leather jacket zipped up. As folks are entering they are taking off their jackets and hanging them up. Someone had asked to take Pat's coat and he refused and walked and took his seat. What was Pat up to thought many of his friends.

[Pat asked the host for a microphone – very carefully not to be noticed]

As the Postmaster came up to the podium and said a few words about Tony and the award he then called up Tony to the podium." Postmaster said, "Today – We honor Tony Lombardo. I present you the ELT Award. Congratulations Tony..."

Tony shook the Postmasters' hand and proceeded to say a few words for the pack filled room who shared this honor with Tony. As Tony walked down from the podium after giving his speech and many claps and laughter from the audience he was met with Pat.

You see Pat was literally standing and waiting for Tony with his microphone in hand... As Tony approached Pat he noticed a huge smirk on this face.

Tony said, "Why do you have your jacket on?"

Pat said, "You got an award tonight but …"

[Pat unzips his jacket – revealing his war medals]

Pat continued to say, "I still have more awards than you! I thought you should know that." Pat had walked away from Tony and hung up his coat and humorously reminded the guests that Pat had more accolades than Tony.

This was the kind of comradery the brothers shared among each other. We were always trying to show each other off.

Annie said, "Tony did I get the story right."

Tony said, "You nailed it, sis."

Pat said to Annie, "I think I survived the war was because of you Annie."

Annie said, "Me? What do you mean?"

Pat said, "Well. One poem in particularly me would always recite in the back of my mind when I was in danger. I think this poem was my lucky rabbit's foot that kept me alive. Do you remember the poem, Annie?"

[Pat recited his poem from 1943]

FAMILY

But for you...
My Mother and Father
I'll fight for this country - much harder
For it's you, I love, and my brothers and sisters
I'll fight like hell
I won't mind blisters
For it's you I love - no one else in mind
Because it's only you
That can be so kind

By Pat Lombardo

Chapter 3:
Operation Raincoat

December 2, 1943
Southern, Italy

Pat said, "Since we now are all here – let's begin to tell our stories from what we endured. But this time there will be no war sensors. I don't know about you my brothers but many of the letters that I wrote seemed upbeat with positivity but the majority of the time it was a miserable time for me. In speaking about war sensors it reminds me of one particular letter that I mentioned a poem called, 'Ode to the Sensor.' Before we get into each of our letters let's start with this particular poem that speaks to our some of our limits of what we can include and not include. Of course, the poem isn't 100 percent true and does have some humor."

Tony said, "Before we go hear it –I miss eating my pound of spaghetti. Can you believe I can still eat a pound of spaghetti in two minutes...? Does anybody want to see me do it? - he chuckled."

[Everyone starred at Tony – the eyes alone knew everyone was anxious to hear the story]

Tony said, "Ok – tough crowd."

[Pat is sorting through the letters]

ODE TO THE SENSOR

Can't write a thing
The sensors to blame
Just say I'm well and sign my name
Can't tell where I came from
Can't mention the date
Can't even number the meals that I've eaten
Can't tell where I'm going
Don't know where I'll land
Can't tell you the name of this foreign land
Can't mention the weather – not even the rain
All military titles must be secret
Can't have a flashlight to guide me at night
Can't smoke a cigarette except out of sight
[Continued]
Can't keep a diary for such is a sin
Can't keep the envelopes your letters come in
Can't be sure just what I can write
So I'll call this a letter and kiss you good
night.

Annie said, "I remember reading this back in the 1940s and it seems like yesterday. Pat pull out one of the letters and read them to us and tell us the untold story from that event. We share would like to know more about your experience."

Pat said, "I would be honored to share the letters in front of my family. I'm glad everyone is here. We are here together and that's what matters most to me."

John said, "I can't believe I'm here with everyone. How much time do we have Vic? I don't want this to end.

Vic said, "Son – don't worry we will have enough time to tell each of our stories."

[Pat reached down and pulled one of the letters from the box]

"ITALY"   December 5, 1943

Dear Sis,
 As you know I haven't written a letter in over 4 days. That's because I didn't receive any for about fix of six days. Today - I did receive six V-Mails. Four from sis, and two from Aggie. I also received a Christmas greeting card from Aggie. I understand Vic was away on liberty. Hope he keeps getting the letters. I only hope he doesn't leave as quickly as I did. Rosey told me he came with a bunch of his shipmates.
    Glad to hear he's making something out of it. How about sending me his address? Sis also tells me John is having a good time in Hawaii. Well, that makes everything just fine. Everybody is in good health. Now, all we have to do is keep our chins up and keep smiling and before long we'll all be together again, just like old times. The Insignia on my army field jacket is supposed to be like this. With an A and a number 5 at the bottom.
                    Love and Kisses
          Always (your kid) Brother - Pat

Pat said, "This letter may sound bland but we couldn't really say much as the mail is censored. The logo that I drew in this letter was the – Fifth Army Unit. During the time of this particular letter, I want to tell you about – Operation Raincoat and some of the battles before during and leading up to the letter so you can understand what I was faced with during this time.

Operation Raincoat was a period when our men had to endure conditions in which we would fight for months to come. With miserable days and nights when rain and show turned every dirt road into a quagmire and fog never left the mountains and the valleys.

Our men struggled on trails too step for even a pack of mules. Everything was tested for the course of the next few months as we prepared for several attacks across the mountain terrain. Our engineering team had to remove train track in order to make a useable road for our trucks to come in and out. The engineers also had to combat with muddy road conditions and spread rock so vehicles would not get stuck in the mud. As it turned out the codename – Raincoat was a fitting name for the operation as rain steadily fell from December 2- 4 1943. We just had received our wool underwear in November and helped us to endure these weather conditions.

During the night, we met with heavy opposition from machine guns and also had to be mindful of enemy minefields and wire which was a constant problem. After the *Capture of the Camino Peaks,* I made my way through *Mount La Remetanea* and by 0945 on December 3rd we captured this territory. However, on December 4th, a counter-attack drove us back from HILL 907 into a defensive position on *Mount la Difensa.*

Just the day before I wrote this letter our Fifth Army Artillery Battalion fired using camouflaged 8-inch Howitzer Cannons into enemy territory. This unit fired an impressive 206,000 rounds stopping by December 4, 1800, hours. During this massive attack, it put a strain on the enemy resulting in many casualties and captures of the enemy. Some of the men that did survive were in a series of caves. This was part of the *Capture of the Main Camino Peaks*. My particular unit was infantry and led us into these peaks, not just these peaks but several were part of our operations. In many of the times, I would write my family letters including Annie – I would be often on patrol and have many sleepless nights.

Annie said, "I always knew being in combat would be risky. Every time I got a new letter from you – I smiled from ear to ear as they would say.

Pat said, "The operation at – The Winter Line especially between Decembers – January was one of the toughest times. I had to endure weather conditions and always remained focused on our missions."

Annie said, "I hate to ask this question – Pat. Did you hesitate when you had to kill anyone – I assume you had to kill – right?"

[Annie gulped in hesitation]

Pat said, "As you know back home, I – We and well everyone really doesn't like talking about the war. This is mainly because it brings back pain and flashbacks from the Good – Bad- and the Ugly as they say. Being in the afterlife – I don't mind sharing with you. We're all here together now. So here it goes.."

It was roughly the 15th of December and we were *On the Road to San Pietro*. We were assisting Company B, 753d Tank Battalion up the road and observed within the range from the left as they progressed through the trials. This was a joint effort between Company A, 636th Tank Destroyer Battalion, and Company C, 753d Tank Battalion. We moved from to support attacks by firing on targets west of San Pietro. A few moments later we received heavy artillery fire and one of the tanks was unsuccessful stuck as they trail became too narrow and un-even for travel. Another factor was avoiding S-Mine's that were planted within close proximity from us. We had lost a few casualties due to these mines within a half mile from our position. The Tanks fired against some Germans including officers from an enemy command post.

My crew was in the midst of taking heavy fire from a machine gun nest at our 4 o clock position. I and units flanked that position while the tank laid down fire. I found myself firing and killing 4 men in and near the machine gun nest. These were my first kills – well kills I know and could see first-hand. You see a lot of prior battles we were stuck in cover and would be spraying bullets but never could tell if we hit anybody as the backup would always arrive. After advancing past this point one of the tanks who crossed the bridge had been disabled by a buried mine. The enemy now laid down heavy artillery and mortar fire down on this area.

Our crew stayed with their tank to fire on any targets appearing on the terraces above the hilly terrain. At that moment an enemy shell exploded against the tank and several us including the ones from the tank.

Our Firth Army unit now joined the troops from 141st infantry as the backup. As we are re-assembling and taking cover against a trench to the right of the tank – A shell set fire to this tank and the other two tanks behind us. As night began to fall only four of the sixteen tanks were able to return back to our assembly area. As Company L and Company E returned to forge forward we were met with the same intense gunfire.

As further units got in the position such as Company G and F – they also received the same wraith from enemy forces. Capt. Charles H Hamner was killed while leaving Company F, and Capt. Charles M. Beacham for Company G was wounded. This battle continued into the next day with intense enemy fire. To sum it up – I was very lucky to come out alive. Especially at the tail end of the many grueling hours of fighting turned into moments to resume wounded comrades. Evacuation and care for our wounded soldiers were difficult due to enemy snipers who fired on the battalion aid station until Company L eliminated the source of the snipers. This was the day that I remember my first confirmed kills. The *Winter Line* was a hard fought battle and I survived to tell about.

Chapter 4: Operation Encore
March 6-9, 1945
Fornaci, Italy

Being in the *Sphere of the Holy Gate* sure does have its perks. For one thing, we are here together and you could drop a tiny pin and it would make the loudest noise. It's so quiet up here and we are so lucky to be united together. I don't want to go back, John had said with much worry.

John Lombardo said to Pat, "Remember your heroism in Italy when you received the Bronze Star Medal. Can you share with us the events that led into that day?"

Pat said, "Of course. I remember this day very clearly. Trench warfare has been infrequent during our time and we didn't really rely on this tactic in our units. It was March 6th and we codename this *Operation Encore* which many allied units assisted in the push forward to overtake the city. We saw units from of the U.S. IV Corps (1st Brazilian Division and the newly arrived U.S. 10th Mountain Division) battling forward across minefields in the Apennines to align their presence to press forward into the city. These units eventually pushed the German defenders from the commanding high point of Monte Castello and the adjacent Monte Belvedere and Castelnuovo, depriving them of artillery positions. Before these units flanked the city we had a task of our own.

We had just walked from the temporary command post which was comprised of military intelligence, small army trucks, and several stations deploying to various locations. I was now on machine gun watch with Jack Barnhart probably about 4000 meters from Monte Belvedere. Let me re-tell the story leading up to the Bronze Star Medal. It was March 6th, 1945 and I and Jack Barnhart were stationed on machine gun data for an undetermined amount of time."

Jack said to Pat, "How long do you think we need to be on watch? It's been 5 hours and I haven't even seen an animal advance down this trail. It's getting dark soon."

Pat said to Jack, "Lower your voice we don't know what's up ahead. Intelligence suggests this trail will lead into advancement further for victory. We can't just storm ahead with any care. It's said up ahead may have a minefield and we're not cleared to forge ahead yet. It's up to us to hold the position in case of an attack."

Jack said to Pat, "Well the good thing is about 900 meters behind us is our temporary command post with reinforcements if we need it. How do you want to handle the sleep situation?"

"Are you kidding me? Our C/O would hang us by the balls if we were to take turns sleeping," – Pat said with much disgust in his voice.

Jack said, "I know these are the orders we must follow – but what if nobody comes to relief us or fill us in. We would be full of exhaustion and defeat."

"What I do know- Is we have a fleet of the 85th Infantry Division will be flanking up this trail from our 1 o'clock. I'm sure we will hear in due time what our next move will be. We are on watch to be prepared for any gunfire up this trail. The 85th knows we are here and if in trouble should lead them up to us and we can take the whole units. These M1919 Browning machine guns we both have will fit nicely down the wide opening about 1200 meters ahead. We got about 1400 meters of range and plenty of ammo. Whoever comes up this trail wish they didn't", Pat said.

Jack said, "Did you name her? I named mine."

Pat looked at Jack and smiled.

Before Pat could answer Jack was rubbing his M1919 Browning machine gun with his hand.

Jack laughed and said, "Think of this as your lady. Nice curves and could penetrate your heart with one look."

Pat said, "You really didn't name your gun, did you?"

"No of course not chuckled Jack. I named my lady. Her name is Irene. You should consider naming yours soon. We are going to be here for a while would be my suspicion so it's time to get close to her", Jack had said.

Pat laughed, "I'm glad that we are here together this will sure pass time, but we need to remain focused at hand."

"Don't change the subject – I want her name," said Jack.

Pat shook his head and said, "If you are that interested her name is Patricia. It's my lady back home – you happy?"

As the sun set temps fell from 60 degrees down to low 40s but this was typical weather that was typical for me being a Hartford, Connecticut native. Jack was a perfect match as he was from Deposit, New York and had no issues with the weather. If I was joined by someone from Florida I'd bet, they would be shivering right now.

Back at the Sphere of the Holy Gate, Annie had interrupted the story for a moment. Annie said, "Did you write any letters while on watch from Italy?"

Pat said, "No – even though the mood and tone could have justified me taking a break – I took my watch very seriously. In the next few days when I was on top of a mountain and out of somewhat danger is when I did write you some letters. Let's go back to the story.

We had many small talk moments for the next 40-50 hours which in total was about 60 hours without any sleep until the first break of action started. It was now March 8, 1945, and our C/O had some news for us. He had mentioned the reminding troops were assisting the 85th to flank the city and other units needed to stay in the command post. He had noted that a member of the 8th Army Unit was under heavy attack and we were the closest unit that could assist. That day we had volunteered to act like a litter team to evacuate a wounded man from an unwept minefield that became under fire from an undetermined amount of enemy soldiers.

The C/O had sent Kendell Casto from Ripely, Virginia to assist us in the evacuation along with 6-7 other friendlies who would eventually be caught up to our six in a few hours from now in case things went sour. Kendell had introduced himself and told us he had a successful mission just a few days ago and was happy to assist in this effort. We had to move out sooner or later so myself and Jack without hesitation agreed.

We pressed up forward as Cpl Hamer and Henry Steadman took our positions on the machine guns. As we progressed up the trail with extreme caution- we moved as one. It was much like a beat of a drum in a rhythmic pattern. Even though there was the three of us – we became one unit as we pushed ahead together. The terrain was rocky with tree lines to the left and right of us. This was the most worried we all have been in a while. We had traveled about 300 meters and stopped to discuss our action plan.

Kendell said to the group, "As we progress up ahead I'll cover the right tree line listening for noises and movement. Who wants to take the center and the left tree line?"

Pat agreed to cover the center of the trail ensuring nothing came into sight posing a threat. That left the left tree line for Jack to cover.

After the game plan had been agreed our unit excelled about 1300 meters up the mountain terrain. Beyond 1300 meters is where the trail had turned from a straight line and into a curve to the left. Right at the curve, we had held a pattern before turning the corner. We sat here for over twenty minutes just listening. This was very important that we tuned everything out and listened attentively. We wanted to be sure we didn't hear any voices or noises that resembled any men around the corner.

Kendell said, "Do you hear that?"

[Faint gunfire was in the distant]

Pat and Jack both agreed they also confirmed hearing what sounded like gunfire.

Jack said, "If we are hearing gunfire from our position as faint gunfire then we still have a way to go but should be cautious. I'm going to lie on my stomach and crawl up to get a sneak peek of what's ahead. I have my binoculars in my bag.

While Jack was getting into position – I covered the rear position and Kendell had covered the tree lines.

Jack had gotten on his stomach and slowly looked with his head around the corner without being seen. He didn't immediately see anything. He then took out his binoculars to confirm anything up ahead. He crawled back to our group.

Jack said, "Guys – I don't see anything up ahead, but it appears the trail turns to the right about 400-500 meters ahead. Let's press ahead carefully."

Our unit formed in the same agreed position and advanced about 200 meters traveling about almost 1500 meters from our original machine gun post. All sudden Kendell had flagged everyone to stop.

Kendell said, "Hold up. With his hand raised in the air- I hear something 3 o clock in the tree line."

Pat had aimed his M41 carbine and was ready for an attack.

Jack had done the same but laid on his stomach and was ready to shoot what would be emerging from the tree line.

Kendell was on one knee dead center and took a closer look at what was making all the noise. Suddenly a deer had emerged from the tree line and ran past the unit.

Kendell had said, "False alarm boys. Let's keep pressing forward."

As we approached the second turn arriving after 300 meters we noticed the terrain was much different as the corner had become available. This time the mouth of the terrain had become a field that was wide open side to side. We proceeded with caution and once again took proper safety measures and Jack had cleared the turn by turning the corner with his M41 raised ready to take fire as he peaked around the corner.

Before Jack had gotten a look, we had heard visible gunfire very close from our position. The once quiet trail now had turned into the sound of flying stray bullets hitting trees up ahead and it was most certainly time for battle.

This time he noticed a US army soldier up ahead who had taken sheltered from a down tree and taking fire. Our group began to strategize the best way to Evac the wounded soldier. With Intel from our C/O we knew that this field could be the minefield they were suggesting which could be fatal for our unit. At the same time, we discussed that if we flanked from the left or right it would take us some time and we would be vulnerable to an attack as we don't have any real cover until we hit the tree line.

Pat said, "I think the best way is right up the middle. Yes, we could be on live minefield, but we don't have time. We can press carefully up the field and if bullets get closer we get down and hold our positions until we reach that fallen tree and rescue our comrade. He's probably no more than 10 minutes from our current position if we advance with caution."

Kendell said, "Once we have him we should advance up the mountain towards the Battalion aid station that the 85th will be advancing down from. We can forge through that tree line up ahead (pointed the way to move). We wouldn't be going back the same way but probably is the best way to get him help and have reinforcements available."

Jack said, "I agree if the men coming behind us realize we are gone they would just press ahead anyway."

Pat said, "Ok. I'm going to move to hand signals. Pat signaled the direction to move ahead and counted down for us to forge ahead."

Our hearts were racing, and we forged ahead and heard more stray bullets being fired but were not in direct line of sight. It almost seemed like the enemy head didn't have a direct line of sight. Without a care in the world, we raced over the open field oblivious that at any moment we could be at the fate of a mine. We had finally reached the wounded soldier behind the fallen tree.

Pat said, "I'm Pat from the 6th Armored Division alongside with Jack and Kendell from Fifth Army Unit. What's your name?"

My name is Kyle. I'm from the 85th Infantry and I'm wounded in my leg and can't walk. Thanks for coming guys. I've been here taking fire for many hours. The rest of my unit forged ahead while I took cover behind this tree. I think it's snipers because it's not steady fire, but I can't tell who's up ahead or maybe its tactical fire to shoot every hour or so. I think they were thinking I would move and maybe they would act upon it," Kyle had said.

Kendell said, "Don't worry Kyle we are here to extract you up the mountain. Probably the same one you came down if you're with the 85th."

Kyle said, "Sounds like a plan but are you sure. That mount is straight up and would take a health man probably a good 5-6 hours for normal conditions. If you carry me this will take us longer to reach our destination."

Jack said, "Kyle – You're right but we can't go back as the best medical treatment for that leg is right up that mountain. Let us worry about the Evac. Let me look at your leg."

Jack had used his knife and cut a piece of his shirt, so he could wrap it around his leg tightly.

Jack said, "This is going to sting but I need to ensure you don't bleed out."

Kendell had covered Kyle's mouth while Pat was checking the surroundings for any movement.

Jack had then securely applied the shirt tightly around his leg while Kyle had screamed but with Kendell's hand over nobody had heard it.

Pat said to the group, "Ok – we are going to move out now. I'll hold cover fire. Jack is going to put you on his back and Kendell will cover us from the rear. You guys ready?

They all shook their heads and they moved out.

As we moved out together as a group Kyle's suspicion was correct it was snipers who must have been watching. Even though they were out of range suddenly things became more dangerous.

In a few seconds later as, our units moved out to the far right were we fired upon with heavy artillery fire from 12/1 o'clock up against the mountain almost dead center. The enemy was watching us and firing their cannons in the hope they would hit us. They had a range of about 1700/1800 feet and came close in hitting us.

As we ran towards the tree line 6-8 rounds per minute from 2-3 different directions came within 10-20 feet from hitting us. As we were running mounds of dirt came rushing up flying in the air with small and large rocks that were hitting us in the face and all over the body. These small fragments felt like a group of bees were invading our body. It was a sound that I never could forget with the ground vibrating while the projectile had hit the ground nearly missing us.

Luckily the adrenaline was in full force we forged ahead to ensure the safety of this mission. Up ahead within 40-50 feet we would hit the same trail that Kyle had once come down. Within just a few minutes we had reached the trail, but we knew the enemy might be coming to ambush us while we retreated to the Battalion Aid Station.

We had stopped when we reached the path up to the mountain for a quick rest and sat down. Suddenly all became quiet. Our unit took deep breaths and Jack had placed Kyle down for a moment while we had a quick chat.

Pat said, "It appears they are using Howitzer's up ahead and now know our position and where we are going. If I was them, I would probably be assembling a unit to traverse and ambush us. We need to be ready."

Kyle said, "This Mountain has rough terrain and uneven terrain. You have more weight when you are carrying me. Be careful not to sprain your ankles. This terrain is unforgiven."

Jack looks up and said, "The only way we are going to pull this off is to take turns with someone watching our backs and 9 o'clock positions."

Kendell said, "I'll take him next and we can change carrying him a few feet at a time with the terrain being so risky. This can be concerning especially if we lose our footing and fall backward. After me – It will be Pat and then Jack, and then me again. If we remain focused and keep working as a unit we will pull this off."

Pat said, "Ok – I'll take rear position while you guys go forward."

As we all stood up we heard gunfire hit the tree lines behind us from stray bullets. In the next moment more, artillery fire hit directly behind us and in the tree line in front us. It didn't they still could not directly reach us, so we forged ahead.

Kendall took Kyle and threw him on his back and began to climb the rocky terrain and each step after each step was carefully planned. The terrain was the most challenging task at hand. After a few feet, Kendell needed to trade off.

We began the task of switching Kyle between each-others back for the next several hours. At that time, I and Jack were the most exhausted especially without sleep for the past 60 hours. Over the next few hours, artillery fire and sniper fire had not been occurring as we approached the steep and rocky terrain.

Just as sunset had begun to go down is when things got very interesting. During this time Pat had Kyle on his back and Kendall had assumed the rear position while we were moving a few feet at a time – Kendell had signaled us to keep moving as he heard rocks or dirt moving from the same very trail they were climbing.

The trail had many turns and terrain to deal with such as fallen trees large rocks and dirt that could swallow your boot due to muddy soaked parts of the trail. Kendell had gotten into position and saw a few enemy soldiers slowly making up the trail.

Kendell had gotten low and took aim.

Kendell had fired and hit one of the German soldiers in the neck with a direct hit. He noticed the other 2-3 start to fire towards him. Kendell returned fire and now was worried they would flank in the adjacent tree line.

Kendell had made a decision instead of going up or taking cover that he would press down towards then. By this time Jack had also made his way back down to assist Kendell.

Pat had dropped Kyle up ahead and was ready to fire from an upwards position.

Jack had assumed the position on the far right of the upper position of the trail while Kendell was moving on the left side.

Kendell saw some movement and fired twice hitting one of the German soldiers on the knee and hand. He screamed in pain and said something in German which probably resembled ~~fuck~~.

Kendell advanced down the trail and arrived to see the German soldier bleeding from the chest. He kicks him. The German didn't move. He picks up the German's hand to examine for a pulse.

The German Solider opened his eyes; grabbed Kendell and front flipped him over his body. He then assumed the top position on top of Kendell.

The German soldier screamed, 'For the Führer." He takes out his knife and is coming down on his chest.

At that moment Jack had been locked in on the German soldier and ready to fire. He aimed and fired but (clicks) due to a gun malfunction.

Pat had advanced down towards Jack's position as he was behind him a few feet and ran towards him for a clean shot. He fired his weapon once locked in and nailed the German soldier above the ear. The impact sent the German soldier to fall onto the cold ground.

Pat stayed with Kyle and Jack ran down to Kendell. Jack helped Kendell up.

Jack said to Kendell, "Are you ok Castro?"

Kendell said, "Yes. ~~God Damn~~ Germans!"

Jack had examined the pockets of the German Solider. He found a few documents on the solider. He confirmed he's dead.

Jack to Kendell, "It's time we re-group with the guys. We have another few hours before we are in the clear."

Kendall said to Jack, "We have to move and continue on. Go back to Pat and Kyle and within 5 minutes I'll move up towards you."

Once again, we all were together and assumed the prior formation and continued to forge ahead up the mountain. From this point forward, we didn't have any further contact from the enemy. It took another ten hours for us to reach the top of the mountain. In total it took our unit fifteen hours and 45 minutes to bring Kyle to safety.

While we reached the top, we were greeted by the medical team who prepared Kyle for treatment to his leg.

Kyle said, "Pat – Kendell – and Jack, I can't thank you enough. You saved my life."

Pat said, "Hang in there Kyle. You're going to be fine."

Jack rubbed his head and said, "Anything for you brother."

Kendell put his hand on his shoulder and said, "You would have done the same. Be well Kyle."

This was the last time we all saw Kyle during World War II. Back at the Sphere of the Holy Gate, "Annie said, I'm very proud of you Pat. You know you are a true war hero. When did you get acknowledged and earn your Bronze Star?"

Pat said, "It became official on June 11, 1945, when M.W Daniel, Brigadier General issued our unit the Bronze Star Medal for our efforts from March 8-9th in Fornaci, Italy.

Annie said, "Yes. I remember this letter in the collection. I believe John has the Official Letter for our actions as I just told. Let's see this letter- I'm excited."

John said, "Sure can. I'm so proud of you Pat."

Pat reads the official letter to the group.

HEADQUARTERS FIRST ARMED DIVISION
APO 251, U.S. ARMY
11 June 1945

SUBJECT: Award of Bronze Star Medal.

To: Pfc, Patrick Lombardo, U.S. Army

The following named enlisted men, Infantry (Armd), Headquarters Company, 6th Armored Infantry Battalion. For heroic achievement in action on 8-9 March 1945 in the vicinity of Fornaci, Italy

These men, members of a machine gun crew, volunteered to act like a litter team to evacuate a wounded man from a minefield. Disregarding the fact that they had been manning machine gun positions for the past sixty hours and had not had any sleep during that time, these men came unhesitatingly to the aid of their wounded comrades and began the dangerous and arduous task before them.

After removing the man from the unwept minefield, it was necessary to carry him over the mountains to the battalion aid station under harassing enemy artillery fire. So steep was the mountain that the only way the litter could be moved was by pushing up the mountain a few feet at a time. Although at the point of exhaustion, the men stuck to their task for fifteen hours and forty-five minutes before finally reaching their destination.

The courage, perseverance, and devotion beyond the call of duty displayed by these enlisted men are credited with saving the life of their wounded comrade and are deserving of the highest praise.

Name	Rank	Service from
Heinrich Hamer	Cpl	Lake Benton, MN
Henry Steadman	Pfc	Moulton, AL
Frank Faccioppi	Pfc	Brooklyn, NY
Patrick Lombardo	Pfc	Hartford, CT
Jack Barnhart	Pfc	Deposit, NY
Jack Norman	Pvt	Charlotte, NC`
Sidney Rick	Pvt	Brooklyn, NY
Leon Hamilton	Pvt	Nelson, IL
Kendell Casto	Pvt	Ripley, WA

Signed,

M.W Daniel
Brigadier General USA
Commanding.

Pat said to Vic, "Where were you in December of 43? Do you remember?"

Vic said, "I do. Hand me the box of the letters and let me go next. I want to read one to you guys and tell you a story. I'm going to call this tale – the Story of Ringworms – Junior – and Feeding the Sharks."

Chapter 5: Ringworms – "Junior" – Feeding Sharks – and Billy

December 17, 1943
U.S. Naval (Radio) School, Bedford PA

Before – I get into the letters about Ringworms – Junior – and feeding the sharks, I wanted to read a letter which was written fifteen days after Pat's letter. Poor Annie – she must have wished she had a secretary with responding and sorting so many letters. This letter shows how anal the US Navy was about their inspections within their rooms. This particular letter I had written to Mom, so Annie may not have heard it before – this is a perfect time.

December 17, 1943

Dear Mom,
I am sorry, I haven't written in so long, but I got into a little bit of trouble. It isn't my fault, but I am in it anyhow. The Captain came into our room and found the room in a general mess. So, our room had to go to the Captain's Mast (on-trail). For punishment, we had a white glove inspection. A white glove inspection means there should be no dust on the floor, behind pipers, corners, dressers, etc. Well, it took us only 2.5 hours to clean the room. He came in and had touched behind the mirror, and I think that's the only place we forgot and his finger caught a speckle of dirt. So we had to go to the Captains Mast again for punishment.

We have "White Glove Inspection," seven nights in a row and if we don't pass seven in a row, we start a new seven again. As punishment, we don't have any liberty until we pass seven in a row. By the way, my procedure mark went from 2.9 to 3.7 on my typing test. I got a 4.0 on my code test. How's that for improvement? Today, I typed 15 WPM and by Thursday I need to do 20 WPM. To tell you the truth I'm really disgusted by this place but I'm still trying my best. You still haven't sent Pats and John's addresses. I received 8$ from Annie. Thank you very much for me and giver her kiss. I am sure puzzled what to get everyone for Christmas. I am going to start taking out ½ my pay which is about $20 a month. Well, I guess I will close now with Love + Kisses. Mom if I ever hear that you keep worrying about us, it would make me feel miserable. So please mom keep your chin up, this was will be over soon.
　　　You're Loving Son,
　　　　Vic

　　Annie said to Vic, "Tough times but you stuck with it."
　Vic said to Annie, "Gee thanks, Sis."
　　John said, "They probably do inspections like this today– I guess traditions never die. Where do Ringworms – Junior – and Sharks come into play?"
　　Vic said, "Oh and don't get me started on Junior."
　　[Vic is shuffling through the letters]
　　Vic said, "Ok – I'm going to read a letter about junior next."

March 7, 1945
Philippines

Dear Sis,
I got up for my watch like a good little boy
and ate a slice of bread and jam with a half
of can of pears. They are Australian pears and
not very good ones. We sure can be thankful
for the wonderful food we have in America.

Bill is getting a Captain Mast for sleeping on
watch. The commander caught him up lying on a
desk and said he was sleeping. I guess you
know I don't get along with my executive
officers; I always make fun of him because he
is so dumb. One day I had to run him out of
our quarters because he woke me up. He is
young too. I don't think he is over 19 years
of age and is about Pat's size. Even the
skipper said he was going to put him in some
little corner somewhere with a piece of paper
and pencil, as that's all he is good for. I
call him "Junior," and that gets him mad. I'd
like to write a book about this navy, and tell
people how dumb most officers are. I know how
many foolish little things he cuts out of my
letters and there is nothing I can do about
it. The staff communication officer is going
to censor this letter as he will realize how
dumb our executive is. I don't think he even
reads my letters – just stamps them.
I close now with Love + Kisses
A special kiss for mom
God Bless
You're Kid Brother Vic

March 12, 1945
Philippines

Dear Sis,

I have a pretty easy watch the next couple of days, which is the 8 to 12 both day and night. I just got off the 12 to 4 and what a lovely watch. We got paid today, I got $27 and I played poker for ½ hour and didn't even win. The communication officer was shooting the breeze with me. I hope he doesn't change as most officers do. A lot of officers seem to be pretty nice guys until they get to know you. I used to get along with our skipper until a while back. I told him what I didn't like about him and he told me what he didn't like about me. So we both are straightened out and now are flying right. Even "Junior" came by and offered a few words trying to be nice. I guess this is all I can think of saying. I know the executive would cut it out. He would cut my throat if he had the chance.
Love and Kisses
You're Kid Brother Vic

Vic said to the group, "You see Junior in my last letter was seeking revenge and boy did he get it. I didn't see it coming. Let me tell you the story leaving off in my last letter. It was me who was dumb in the end."

Junior had walked over to me on the deck that night and got the best of me. I underestimated him.

Junior said to Vic, "Hey Vic – I know people talk and say things about my ability to command this ship. How dumb I am or how young I am. I'm sure you have heard this before?

[Before I could answer]

Junior said, "Well it doesn't matter. What does matter is I'm here to congratulate you."

Vic with a confused face said, "Come again. Congratulate me for what?"

Junior said, "Well truth be told this job is tough as nails. For Christ sake, we are at war. This job – my job – all of our jobs can be – well let's say not acknowledged. So you see- I'm here in peace with this un-opened bottle of Calvert Special Whiskey. I say this calls for a toast. We just docked and are on liberty for the next day or two."

Vic looked perplexed at such a motion but agreed to share a drink with the once called – dumb officer.
Vic said, "Sure why not. Yes, pour me a glass of that American whiskey. It's sure better than having any more Australian pears."

We had both laughed at that moment. This was refreshing because I did not care for Junior.

Junior had distracted Vic by dropping something on the deck. While Vic was retrieving it – Junior had turned his back and poured a drink for Vic. He had reached and poured some type of substance in the glass without Vic's knowledge.

Junior said, "Thanks for picking that up for me – that's my favorite compass. He hands Vic the cup of whiskey. Cheers."

[Glasses chime]

For the twenty minutes we were just talking like men – not to worry about rank or size of your ~~balls~~. Just men. At that moment it hit me and I felt dizzy. I fainted to the ground.

I remember waking up with a massive headache like someone threw me in a boxing match. As I looked around I appeared to have been shoved into one of the spare rescue boats with a blanket hiding me.

I realized I was missing for over 3 hours and 40 minutes and missed my watch. Bill had stumbled upon Vic waking up and was worried to death about him.

Bill said, "Vic where have you been? You were supposed to be on Watch a few hours ago? Junior was looking for you and probably will have you report to the Captain.

Vic said, "I'll tell you after. I underestimated Junior. In that moment Junior had the biggest dumbest smirk on his face and stopped to talk to Vic.

Junior said, "Come with me to talk to the captain."

That's when I realized for once "Junior" had gotten me back big time. I made it to the Captain's chambers and didn't dare tell him what had really happened. How dare I to accuse an executive officer of drugging me? I kept it simple.

The captain said to Vic, "What happened?"

Vic said, "I'm sorry sir – I had too much to drink and lost track of time." He handed me a piece of paper.

MEMORANDUM FOR OFFICER OF THE DECK

Subject: Mast Reports.

1. The following punishments were awarded a Captain's Mast held this date at 1030.

LOMBARDO, Vic – S2C. OFFENSE: Drunkenness while on liberty. AOL for 3 hours 40 minutes. PUNISHMENT: Lose 1 liberty.

I read the paper and handed it back to the Captain and Acknowledged and signed the offense. On my way out after turning the coroner it was Junior who stood dead center in the corridor. He was staring at me. As I approached closer he stopped me with his arm on my shoulder. He turned his head and said, "Who's the dumb one now."

Vic replied to Junior and said, "You are Junior, I told the captain everything. How you drugged me. The medical team will be confirming this and you will get transferred due to your cowardly act. Who's the dumb one now?"

Junior locked eyes with Vic and said, "Bullshit."

Junior stormed off towards the direction of the captain's office. This was the last time I saw Junior.

Annie laughed with much conviction to Vic. She turned to Vic and said, "What do you think happened to him? It sounds like he fell for your bait. You sure got even with him. Well done Vic."

Vic said, "That's not something you can ask about. We are just small minnows in the navy and wouldn't dare to ask a senior officer these questions. The only thing we hear is the rumor mill. I had heard from some of the other shipmates that he was taken away."

Annie said, "Taken Away? What did you hear happen to Junior?" with an interested look on her face.

Vic said, "Well – you see in the Navy we always have some sort of drills to occupy time. While we are at war we must still have training exercises. One week maybe its depth charges or ammo drills and so forth – we always need to be ready for war. One particular day I heard from one of our radiomen in the communication room when we had a drill. He mentioned he saw Junior discreetly being escorted off when the LCT 963 delivered our mail with a hoist and pulley system. It was said that while our men were getting the mail he slipped off with the military police in the same vessel."

Annie said, "What do you think Junior is doing now in present day if he was still alive."

Vic laughed and said, "Well that's easy. If Junior were alive he'd be working where all the nuts are."

Annie shook her head, "What do you mean?"

"Well, of course, he'd be working in management at a hardware store. He'd fit right in with all the nuts and bolts in the store as he was a few nuts and bolts short of being anything else," Vic said.

John Lombardo said, "Vic – Here is another letter dated May 21, 1945. It's badly damaged and mentions a fight involving a crew member and the cook. Do you remember this story? "

Vic chuckled and said, "Another Billy Moment – is what I would call it."

Annie said, "Do tell us about Billy and the cook." Annie looked at Vic with much interest.

Vic said, "You see one day it was I and Billy were small talking on the main deck. We didn't notice the cook behind us. Let's just say Billy bad talked the cook and things went sour.

[Vic Reads letter]

March 21, 1945

Dear Sis,
Just got back from a show. Saw "Strike up the Band," with Mickey Roonie. I've seen it before a long time ago, but it was worth seeing it again. We saw it at the Army Engineers. Last night on the LST we saw, "Return of the dead man." It was very good also. Neither of them was war films, so that made them extra well. The cook and Billy had a fight in the Galley. I guess Billy got the worse of it, he had a big notch over his left eye and the cook's teeth marks were all over his hands. Yes, the cook bites when he fights. Both of them claim the other struck him when his back was turned. Both of them lie like a rug. Anyhow both of them are happy again and they've forgotten the whole matter.

We talked to a soldier in the movies tonight for a while and he said in the news tonight from General McArthur that the war here will only be a matter of a few weeks. I asked him if he knew McArther well, and he said no. I told him the things I've heard from the crew. I guess I talked him out of the war ending soon. As you know I'm not very good at writing long letters so I will end with. Special Kisses for Mom –
   Kid Brother
   Vic

"While we were on the main deck on the LST – Billy and I were having a conversation and the cook walked past us while Billy was critiquing his food," Vic had said.

[61]

[Vic explains the story]

Billy to Vic, "I can't believe how bad the food is here. Our cook cannot cook. I'd rather eat Australian peaches and dead cockroaches over these soggy mashed potatoes."

[While Billy is saying this the cook is walking behind him]

Vic said, "Come on. They aren't that bad."

Cook [Takes metal tray] and hits Billy. You don't like potatoes – huh, he said with disgust.

By this time several seamen began to crowd around the men.

[CROWD] surrounds them to watch

Billy had tackled him to the ground and hits him in the face with his fist.

Of course, the cook didn't like that so he grabbed his hand and bites his hand.

After this commotion occurred it received the attention of the executive officers rather quickly.

Lt. Commander [breaks up the fight] orders them to captain mast.

Both of the men were sent to The Captain Mast immediately to explain the situation, Vic had said.

Captain Edwards is pacing back and forth and was speaking to Billy and the Cook. He said, "Unbelievable!! We are in the midst of war and you two are acting like children. Outside right now.. In our sky — below us in the water- our enemy is laughing at us. Why are we fighting each other and not the enemy?"

Billy said defending himself, but Captain...

Captain Edwards abruptly interrupted him. Excuse me. Don't interrupt me when I'm asking Rhetorical question! Now I'm not one to cus' but I heard it was because you didn't like how the fucking mashed potatoes tasted. Fucking potatoes? I'll tell you what son - I've had the potatoes and there isn't anything wrong with them. Now, are we going to have any future issues between you two?

Captain Edwards with much authority in his voice said "Go to medical and get your arm checked out for those bite marks and Charlie the same for you your cut under your eye.

Punishment as served: 1 day of solitude in the Fox Hole for both. Dismissed."

"The other factor we needed to combat in the South Pacific was ringworms," Vic had said. I actually got infected on my leg as I'll be reading the next letter for further context on the matter. Dermatophytosis, also known as ringworm, is a fungal infection of the skin. Typically it results in a red, itchy, scaly, circular rash.

Feb 5, 1945

Dear Sis,
I received your short letter; it was so short
it looked like one of mine. You say it was 10
below zero in Hartford? I didn't know it ever
got cold in Hartford. Where I went to school
up in Pennsylvania it was 20 below mostly all
of the time, but it was a dry cold. You're
bowling scores are improving. If you get much
better I'll be afraid to play you for
stickers. By now mom should have her coat,
don't forget to take a picture of her in it
and send it to me. I haven't got a picture of
mom with me. I have ringworms on my leg now,
and they are very itchy. The doc put some
purple stuff on them, and when I took my
shower it rubbed off, so I put some quinsana
on them and they don't itch anymore, but they
feel to be like they are on fire. We got a
couple of those shots the other day. I don't
know what they were for, but one of them made
my arm sore. Last night I went to the movie
and there was no sound so we didn't see a
picture. I go again tonight and they only had
sound through 1/5 of the picture. Anyhow there
was a pretty girl in the picture. The name of
the picture was, "My heart belongs to daddy."
I close now with loads of love and kisses.
Special kisses for mom + pop. Tell pop to have
a drink on me. - Kid Brother - Vic

"I know it's here somewhere," Vic had said while sorting through the box of letters. Annie said, "What are you looking for."

"It's a particular letter about feeding sharks and much more. I basically beg the Japanese to surrender. You'll see and could imagine how much we hated the enemy. So in the letters, we write with much haste towards them," Vic had said.

Vic shouted with all his might and said – "I found it."
[Vic starts reading the letter]

May 24, 1945
LCT 1091

Dear Sis,
Received quite a few letters today, but none from you (naughty girl). This is the second time we got mail since we've been here. We got some bananas from the natives a couple of days ago, and you should see how big they are. Well, they're one foot long and 2.5-inch diameter. I doubt you will ever see them that size in the states. A couple of hours ago we saw some sharks swimming around our LCT, so we threw them some meat and they really jumped for it. This is always some way to have a little fun around here. Now whoever thought I would be throwing meat to sharks! This is certainly making a lot of changes, isn't it?

I hope the Japs quit before all of them are killed because it will take an awfully long time to kill all of them, it is best to kill all of them though, so they won't be around to start another war in 20 years. We are getting underway now for another assignment, we no longer drop our anchor and have to pick her up again. At least we are doing our share to help win the war. I'll probably get home in the middle of winter, and will I be cold.

I guess after getting a custom to the warm climate I can get used to the cold again. I'd probably be complaining all the time if I was in the Pacific. Well correction, I mean the Atlantic. One of these LCT's you don't have hardly any place to go keep warm when it gets cold. I am feeling pretty good lately. No trouble, no stomach aches, and I've been doing pretty good on getting sleep. I think I will close now and get more sleep. Good Night.
    Special Kisses for Mom
    God Bless You
    Vic

Chapter 6: Mutiny

LCT 1092 whom had 200 Japanese soldiers along with the 50 US Army 103rd Infantry Division as part of Operation Merchant

John had spoken to the group - its funny how you're worried what the mail censor will send out and not send out due to regulations of sorting the mail and deeming what's acceptable and what's not acceptable. I'm holding a letter in my hand that I wrote to the Sis & Family involving two Japanese bills that were soaked in blood. You have to remember during the war - we hated the Japanese and often collected souvenirs as a reminder of the war.

Sept 16, 1944
Pacific

Dear Sis & Family,
I am enclosing two Jap bills that Lando gave me to send to you. They are worth two dollars and a half each. One of them has a shrapnel hole and blood of one of his Marine buddies, that's in the company he used to be in. Boy, he really looks good though. He hasn't changed a bit. Just the same as he ever was. He had the duty yesterday, so he couldn't get liberty. If he did get off, we were going to go see Joe La Rose, because Joe was over to see the other day, and Joe gets Sundays off. In fact, none of us there got off the same day. From the looks of things, it looks like as if Tony has been throwing some pretty good parties. Well, I guess you better learn how to skate sis, because you know they were made to skate on. Words are failing, so I'll have to close with..

Love + Kisses
God Bless You & Family

```
You're Loving Brother + Son
"Lumps"
John Lombardo MM 4/c
     (Page 3- Next Day)

Instead of writing a whole new letter, I'll
just add this page. By the time you'll see
that the Jap money isn't in the envelope.
That's because the letter was sent back to me,
and the censor said I couldn't send them.
Today was Joe La Rose's liberty day, so he
came over here and spends the day with me, and
tonight I took him over to see Lando. Boy,
they sure were glad to see each other. So I
gave him the bills back to Lando. Here they
are only about a quarter of a mile from each
other, and y
John Lombardo MM 2/c
```

    John had said to the group, "As you can see mail censorship was necessary and some items went through circulation and some did not. What many civilians didn't understand that for many of us young men this was our first adventure being independent? So taking orders from other's and still having a rebellious type of blood was hard to restrain sometimes. As you heard earlier from Pat not every day we are upbeat and happy to be in accompany with our crew and or officers. This reminds me of a story that Tony had told about Mutiny. He can explain it better than I could. Often time's morale could impact one's decisions which remind me of a story that occurred on July 17, 1944, involving Mutiny.

Mutiny is a criminal conspiracy among a group of people (typically members of the military or the crew of any ship, even if they are civilians) to openly oppose, change, or overthrow a lawful authority to which they are subject. The term is commonly used for a rebellion among members of the military against their superior officers, but it can also occasionally refer to any type of rebellion against authority figures or governances.

[Flashback Sept, 1945 on Mindanao Island]

Sailor to Tony, "Welcome to Mindanao Island we have ammo and supplies and some men that will be transported?"

Tony, "Why the Men?"

Sailor said to Tony, "We will transport 20 of the Japanese soldiers and 50 of the US army 103rd infantry onto the DE528."

Tony said, "Why is it the Japanese smell worse alive than dead? What are we doing with these Japs?"

Sailor Chuckles, "You try spending a week with them in your boat. Talk to the captain – it's for Operation Merchant."

Tony said, "Twenty of them? I thought we had 30 Jap soldiers."

Sailor said, "We do."

Tony said, "Where is the rest going?"

Sailor with a deeply concerned voice, "I shouldn't be telling you this- Did you hear the story a few months ago on May 1945? Captain Marvin Watkins and an unknown number Air Force crew boarded their B-29 Super fortress bomber. They were shot down and the American's thought they were being treated on foreign land for their injuries."

Tony said curiously, "No, I have not heard this story."

Sailor said, "Well – it's said the Japanese experimented on our men. Intelligence suggests that the Japanese ate part of the brain and livers of soldiers. They were dissected while they were alive. Other experiments were the injection of seawater into their blood at university's medical school."

Tony said with much emotion, "Let me guess the Captain is not found of this story. Perhaps he has something special planned for the ten Japanese."

Sailor said, "You see in the Japanese culture it's rumored that when you ask for a volunteer whether it's a kamikaze mission or otherwise and you don't aid it's dishonorable for them to say no. Just the same with any mutiny or disobeying an order – the commanding officer could literally kill you right then and there. So, when you ask what the Captain will do – we aren't animals here Tony.

Tony with a concerned voice said, "Well the captain just asked for a large amount of extra fuel. He's going to burn them to death - I have a bad feeling."

Sailor said, "If the Captain ordered you to pour fuel on them and light a match – would you do it? "

Tony with a raised voice said, "Of course, an order by a commanding officer must be followed. It's like the story of Mutiny dating back to July 17, 1944. Do you remember this?"

Sailor said, "I've heard about it."

Tony explained the story and said, "The Port Chicago Mutiny involved African American enlisted men in the U.S. Navy who refused to return to loading ammunition after a disastrous explosion at Port Chicago, California on July 17, 1944, that destroyed the Liberty ship, SS E.A. Bryan. Sailors and dock workers were pressured by time and their superiors and were also using unsafe unloading methods. These methods, all common practice on munitions docks at the time despite their danger, led to a munitions ship explosion that killed all the Navy men on the E.A. Bryan and many Navy dock workers on shore.

All told, 320 sailors, 202 of whom were African Americans, were instantly incinerated in the explosion. The blast wave was so powerful it could be felt as far away as Boulder City, Nevada, 430 miles to the south and caused damage 48 miles away in San Francisco. The force of the explosion launched massive chunks of debris, some of which fell almost two miles from ground zero. The falling debris injured another 390 people. The Port Chicago explosion was by far the worst disaster on home soil during World War II.

When Navy replacement sailors were asked to return to loading munitions a month later, 258 African American enlisted personnel refused to follow the order. They wanted Navy officials to change load procedures to enhance safety. When the Navy refused to amend its procedures, the sailors declared they would not load the ships. Those who refused the order to load ammunition said that they would follow any order, save the one to do unsafe work under these conditions. Naval officials declared a mutiny and had most of the men arrested.

Two hundred eight of these men were court-martialed, sentenced to bad conduct discharges, and the forfeit of three month's pay for disobeying orders. Fifty of the men, however, were charged with outright mutiny, a crime punishable by death. They would be known as the Port Chicago 50. No Port Chicago sailor convicted of mutiny was sentenced to death; however, most were sentenced to eight to fifteen years of hard labor. In January of 1946, however, all of the accused were given clemency and were released from prison.

As the war came to a close, changes to the loading procedures finally came, ironically mostly due to the Port Chicago explosion and subsequent protest. The Navy recognized that its black sailors performed the vast majority of ammunition ship loading and unloading in segregated units with low morale and often led by bigoted or incompetent officers. The vast majority of these sailors, according to National Association for the Advancement of Colored People (NAACP) investigators, saw themselves as little more than expendable laborers working under egregious conditions.

These revelations prompted Navy officials to start to work towards full desegregation of their personnel by 1945, three years before President Harry Truman issued Executive Order 9981 which integrated the Armed Forces.

The Port Chicago explosion and mutiny proved to be a pivotal point for the decision made within the Navy to desegregate its ranks. In 1994 the Port Chicago Naval Magazine National Memorial was dedicated to those who lost their lives in the disaster." For the next few days, we had boarded the AVB-10 and were on route to rescue and repair Infantry landing craft (gunboat) LCI(G)-404 who was damaged by suicide swimmers, in Yoo Passage, Palaus

Tony on the machine gun said, "If I see any other vessel near the LGI-404, I'm going to take this single 20 mm cannon and blast them away."

Navy Sailor said, "You know you're not supposed to be on the gun. Our jobs are to evocate and repair. What if you accidentally discharge the weapon? Aren't you afraid of a negligence discharge?"

Tony said, "You never wanted to just squeeze the trigger and blast the japs away into pieces?

Navy Sailor said, "I haven't thought about it but we all have a purpose."

Tony said, "Ok let's get ready to board the LGI-404."

Chapter 7: Mindanao Island
Jan 9, 1945
Mindanao Islands, Philippines

Tony said to the group at the Sphere of the Holy Gate, "I have a great story to tell you about the tension between the crew and superior officers. This is about Lt. Commander O'Connor."

My name is Tony Lombardo. We weren't allowed to drink beer on the ships. When we arrived at Mindanao Island we were authorized to drink on the island. On the island, we would meet up with other officers and enlisted crew of the US Navy and US army. This is the day I ran into Lt. Commander O'Connor for the first time. Tony is walking with Lt. Commander Ronald Harper. He was stopped by Lt. Commander O'Connor. Tony has beer in a plastic cup full to the rim.

Lt. Commander O'Connor to Tony Lombardo, "Ensign: I order you to give me that beer, right now."

Tony with disgust, "No- I'm not giving you my beer. Absolutely not! I don't report to you!!"

Lt. Commander O'Connor: (Pushes him with his finger) and said, "Ensign, I'm going to teach you some manners. Let's go to the training barracks right now. That's an order. Do you have any idea who my father is?" Lt. Commander O'Connor had walked away.

Tony said to his Lt. Commander, "Do you know who his father is."

Lt. Commander Harper said, "I have no idea."

Lt. Commander O'Connor came back into view and slapped the cup of beer out of Tony's hand. He said, "That's an order!"

At this moment we had walked into the training barracks and followed Lt. Commander O'Connor per his request.

Lt. Commander O'Connor said, "It's time to teach you some manners. Why do you need your XO here? "

Lt. Commander O'Connor pushes the other Lt. Commander to the floor.

Tony had put my hand out and helped my XO up. Its ok I'll handle this for you. I know what to do Tony had said.

Lt. Commander O'Connor didn't know that I had been boxing since the 6th grade and that was my sport in High School and I was pretty good. I looked at the Lt. Commander notice he was a pretty stocky fellow. Boy here is where I get the crap beat out of me. Well Maybe? Tony got into a boxing stance. Got his feet planted.

Tony said almost yelling, "This is where I teach you some manners."

Lt. Commander O'Connor pushed me and said, "Let's go. Make your move."

Tony pulled his arm back while tightening his fist and threw a hard punch square in the Lt. Commander's chest. This resulted in the Lt. Commander falling to his knees.

Lt. Commander O'Connor was holding his chest and in pain and on his knees

Tony landed a right cross against his face. After throwing the punch, I was in pain. This is the day I broke my hand on his face).

Lt. Commander O'Connor had fallen to the ground.

Lt. Commander O'Connor said, "I've had enough while holding his face."

Lt. Commander O'Connor brings himself back up to a standing position and said, "My ship leaves tonight and I'll be back tomorrow. I'm ordering you to fight me in an unsanctioned fight. I'll be back tomorrow. I don't care you brought your XO here to be a witness in this matter. My father is a Rear Admiral so ask yourself – Who are they going to believe what happened? You two or me? I can ruin your life in four minutes.

Tony said, "I hurt my hand. I think it's broken."

Lt. Commander O'Connor shouts, "I don't care. Put it on ice and I'll be back tomorrow around this time to train and then fight you." On the way out Lt. Commander O'Connor shoulder checked me and was pissed I defeated him. [The Next Day, Mindanao Islands]

Tony was boxing with left hand on the bag. His right hand is taped. He then puts on his right glove and gingerly hits the bag with box hands.

Lt. Commander O'Connor walked into the training facility.

Lt. Commander O'Connor looked at Tony and shook his head. He took out a brass button from his pocket. He took a moment and stared at it like it was his mortal enemy. He then gazed over at Tony and took aim. He threw it at Tony and it hit him. Tony was not amused and didn't even look over. This infuriated the Lt. Commander.

In preparation of training Lt. Commander O'Connor begun to take his jacket off. He started to punch the bag and thought of Tony's face.

Tony said, "He stopped for a moment and gazed over at me. He gave me a big smirk but I was not allowing him to get in my head."

We had made our way into the training boxing ring at our barracks. I had my fellow sailors cheering me on beyond the ropes. It was no surprise that Lt. Commander O'Connor didn't have any support. I was thinking he was probably hated on his ship. The bell was rung and we began the fight. I had started to press forward towards Lt. Commander's corner but he drew me back with a few jabs. He threw a few hard punches but I blocked them. He looked angry and immediately began to fight dirty. I wasn't surprised. Lt. Commander O'Connor threw a knee to my leg and pressed me back towards the ropes. I could hear my fellow sailor's cheer me on as they were chanting, "Tony." I could also hear them say, "Dirty shot," in reference to the knee he had thrown at me.

While I was holding my leg in pain it had opened up a hole for Lt. Commander O'Connor to attack. He immediately took advantage and threw some hard body shots to my rib cage. I reacted with a short punch to his face that drew him back. This gave me my chance. I then threw a hard right cross to his face. It connected and he fell to the ground. I could hear my fellow sailors say, "You aren't so pretty now."

Lt. Commander O'Connor was on the ground holding his face and jaw.

Tony had approached O'Connor with arms raised but then puts his hands out and helps him to his knees.

Lt. Commander O'Connor while out of breath said, "You're pretty good.

Tony (Gives Smirk) and said, "Next time you will get your own beer. You understand me...Sir?"

Lt. O'Connor said, "My name is Sebastian. Ensign, I never got your name?"

Tony said with much authority in his voice, "It's Tony. Tony Lombardo."

Lt. O'Connor said, "If you ever want to work under me put in a transfer. I'd be honored to have you on my ship."

Tony had said, "One condition.."

Lt. O'Connor looked with interest and said, "Anything."

Tony with a humorous tone said, "My XO is ~~pissed~~ that you pushed him. He told me you push like a girl and wants to fight you."

Lt. Commander gave a head nod while laughing and walked out of the ring.

THIS IS THE DAY I became friends with Lt. Commander O'Connor.

Today was the last day we were stationed at Mindanao Island while we fixed some neighboring ships. We also loaded them with fresh ammo, mail, and fruit. The boxing was something that allowed us to put our minds at ease. I and Lt. Commander O'Connor allocated a room behind the boxing

Lt. Commander, "What's your secret?"

Tony said, Secret? What do you mean?"

Lt. Commander said, "You've been boxing since the 6th grade. You're pretty ~~damn~~ good. How did you become so good?"

Tony explained himself. Have you ever put a hamster in a maze and watched one in a maze?

Lt. Commander replied, "No – I haven't"

Tony said, "The hamster will begin to developing memory based on where it's gone. What wall was a dead end? This helps the hamster to find the exit. It studies its surroundings but not just studies it – the creature remembers subtle things. Much like boxing; I let my opponent lead for a while. I start to follow a pattern and remember it. Then I find vulnerability and I attack."

Lt. Commander had said, "You and I are much the same. You seem to strategize more – I like that." While we were getting to know each other we noticed a big man who was watching us.

The man who was watching us picked his way through the sailors who made a full circle around us. He pushed them aside like rag dolls. He was known as the "Champ."

The Champ said, "You guys couldn't beat a real fighter like me."

Tony & O'Connor had turned to each other with amusement. Tony said to O'Connor, "I'm going to shut him up. "O'Connor pushed Tony while tensely saying, "No, I want to fight him."

Tony had pushed O'Connor and he pushed me back. We did this as a distraction to the champ being confused about who is fighting him. As we continue to fight and push each other at that moment the champ had moved within close proximity to us.

Tony diverted his conflict with O'Connor and immediately hit the champ with a body shot. This was followed by a snapping right cross from O'Connor to the Champ's face. The champ had growled with anger. The champ re-acted with a front kick that landed Tony back into the crowd. Tony fell down holding his stomach in pain.

O'Connor had then attempted a few punches but they were blocked by the champ. The champ pushed O'Connor into the crowd like they were ropes.

While being pushed by some of the champ's friends back into the fighting circle O'Connor was met with a full clothesline and was knocked out. He was dragged behind the circle by his fellow sailors.

Tony had returned visibly into the ring and threw a punch that was blocked by the Champ. The Champ immediately grabbed Tony by his hair and head-butted him. Tony had fallen to his knees due to impact. While on the ground, I had the opportunity to make my mark.

Tony had landed two punches to the knees of the champ with these blows putting a hurt look on his exterior face. As I came up I throat checked him with my fist and then immediately returned with a knee to the face. This was the day we defeated, "The Champ."

Chapter 8: Leon Grabowsky

March 15, 1945
Norfolk, VA

Annie said to Tony, "Didn't you meet Leon Grabowsky?"

Tony said, "Yes I did let me tell you a story dating back to March 15, 1945. I'll tell my story and as if it was Leon was telling the story.

The USS Mason assembled in Norfolk, VA for a secret mission, "Operation Merchant."

We were assembled on the USS Mason which just came back to the port which comprised of mostly African-American crew. I was called to the USS Mason – DE-528 for new orders. On this day we assembled on the Fan Tail position of the ship where Leon had introduced himself to us and my fellow shipmates.

My name is Leon – and I'm very much like everyone that stands next to you. You see this book [holds up the bluejacket manual] where we are going this book will not do you any good. We are about to operate on the USS Mason for a short time until we reach our destination. When we reach our destination, you might as well throw this book out [throws book]. Our mission is designated as "Operation Merchant." You will be debriefed the finer details in due time.

Now, look around the deck of who accompanies us here today. We are nothing- nobody- and piles of garbage. We are equals. At this moment- we have been brought to Norfolk as strangers. I say these things because I once had these same feelings. A few things entered my mind such as today in your minds. What is my purpose? Could I perform my watch as warranted? I will promise you this. As we enter this journey together we shall embark the respect of me and every single man on this ship. We will look out for each other and stand together as a unit.

This is a marriage with the ultimate commitment of love. Love for each other must be strong and we are now a family on this day and many days out at sea.

I may be your captain and I see every one of you looking at me with doubt and regret. Yes, I'm young – but these eyes and hold a secret- a secret some of you may never experience. Some may say my inexperience may be the death of us.

I'll tell you a little story. How many of you here today know the name of Leon Grabowsky?

I am Leon Grabowsky

[People mumbling and talking.]

I see now I have your immediate attention. For those who don't know me – where I have been – endured – let this story take hold of my reputation and experience as your captain. By the end of this story, I'll give you two choices. You stand today with me and enter this vessel as a family or you leave immediately as a coward if you still don't believe in my ability to lead this ship. It was February 17, 1945, and I was the Lt. Commander on the USS Leutze. Leutze along with the cruise Pensacola returned fire on the Japs who were firing on the minesweepers. Pensacola was hit several times by artillery fired from Mt Suribachi. Next, Leutze, along with other destroyers with UDTs aboard, moved close to the beach near Suribachi to launch and protect the UDTs as they cleared the beach of obstacles.

The Jap fire was severe from the beach areas as well as from Mt. Suribachi. The destroyers counter fired and the LCI group launched their rocket attack. Within 10 minutes, an artillery or mortar shell from Mt. Suribachi struck Leutze's forward stack area, damaging boilers #1 and #2 and seriously wounding Captain Robins and three crewmen. Leutze's counter fire continued as Lt. Grabowsky, the XO, relieved Captain Robbins who lay paralyzed on the starboard wing of the bridge. He was wounded and was transferred for needed medical care.

We were under intense fire from the beach. Mortar shells were falling all around us; five-inch shells, three-inch shells, you name it. During such time – I assumed command while we were under intense attack. I was able to gather resources to control the situation.

The next morning, 18 February, Leutze and another destroyer began escorting the battleship New York to Ulithi for evaporator repairs. While in Ulithi, Leutze had a tender availability to repair battle damage. Leutze returned to Iwo Jima on 6 March and participated in called fire until departing on 10 March when DesRon 56 destroyers began departing for Ulithi.

On the sixth of April, a three-hundred-plane suicide attack came in. It was the main attack. Many were shot down by Task Force 58 fighters, but a whole swarm of them got through. The heavy ships formed up west of Okinawa. We were ordered into the screen from the fire support station on a twelve-thousand-yard circle.

Only two destroyers got there while the attack was going on--the NEWCOMB and the LEUTZE. They were in Station One, around 30 degrees on the bow of the force. We were twelve to twenty thousand yards from the main force and there was no support from the heavy ships.

This main group of suicides came in on the NEWCOMB and us. We shot down two of them. The NEWCOMB shot down several and then she was hit by four in a row. She was the flagship of our squadron, Commodore Stroop was in command. I went over to pick up survivors. I didn't think there would be anything but scraps of metal left--flaming metal--but the goddamn ship hadn't sunk. So, what to do next? I said, "Well, we will try to save the ship."

It was just before sundown when I felt she was going down. So I brought the LEUTZE in, backed down full alongside the NEWCOMB, and started giving her the hoses and handy-billies they needed to fight the fires. The crew was congregated on the bow and the stern. The center of the ship was a shambles, all in flames. This went on for around ten minutes and we controlled the fires pretty much. Then one last solitary kamikaze was spotted on the other side of the *Newcomb*, coming in low on the water. I didn't have time to cut the lines or anything. It was too late to do anything, so I said, "Shit, I better just stay here and let these guys get on the *Leutze*." That was the safest thing to do. That way we would be screened by the *Newcomb* from damage.

The kamikaze guy came in and hit where the flames were and skidded across the deck, plunging overboard between the two ships under our stern. A five-hundred-pound bomb was aboard the plane and it blew up. Then we were in trouble! Everything aft of the engine room was flooded. The chief engineer was a real smart guy and through real ingenious damage control he and his men shored everything up and saved the steering engine room. There was enough floatation left that the ship didn't sink from lack of floatation, but it was very close. The deck was awash back aft.

Finally, I had to break away and call the task force commander and tell him I had to leave and to send someone to help the NEWCOMB because she still was in trouble. Both ships were saved; we were towed into Kerama Retto by a minesweeper and spent three months there waiting for repairs. One shaft was completely out of commission... That was the story of the LEUTZE. I got the Navy Cross and a lot of others got medals for the operation. There were thirteen Navy crosses in my class. I also received A Bronze Star for Surigao Straits.

And I have three Commendation Ribbons and the Meritorious Service Medal.

I'm supposed to be with the LEUTZE bringing it back for repairs. Today, 01 of September 1945 - I'm with you today on this new secret mission called, "Operation Merchant," with this new fine crew.

I'm your Captain. Any questions

[The crew] shook their head..

Chapter 9: Operation Merchant
Sept 02, 1945
Norfolk, VA

I was invited to a room adjacent from the, "Operations Room," on 02 Sept of 1945 to discuss the new mission from our new appointed Captain. While looking around the room Tony Lombardo was surprised that it was only he and a group of 10-12 others who were selected by Leon Grabowsky for Operation Merchant. Leon had entered the room with what it appeared to be a Rear Admiral of the US Navy.

Leon Grabowsky in attendance with Rear Admiral O'Connor had entered the room.

Leon with the straightest face said to the group, "How do we win this war?"

All twelve of us looked at each other wondering if he wanted a response from us. One of the sailors then said, "Sir. We must kill all of the Japs. By air, land, and sea it must be a coordinated attack."

Leon Grabowsky said, "Wrong. Let me introduce, Rear Admiral O'Connor. We both have been discussing where we as the US Navy from the Sea have fallen short. Does anybody want to try this again?"

Leon Grabowsky said once more, "How do we win this war."

Tony Lombardo had replied, "Sir. We need to know where they have been; where they are doing; and a log of events would help us know. Being one step ahead of them is key."

Leon Grabowsky said, "Exactly. Get this man a beer. I'm going to turn the conversation over to Rear Admiral O'Connor. He's going to discuss some of the things he saw in Okinawa. Sir, please the floor is yours.

Read Admiral O'Connor who was pacing back and forth said, "Leon thank you. Our biggest problem is Intel. Let me re-phrase. The lack of good Intel. This is why myself and Leon Grabowsky will be executing, "**Operation Merchant**," effective 02 Sept 1945.

The naval campaign against Okinawa began in late March 1945, as the carriers of the BPF began striking Japanese airfields in the Sakishima Islands. To the east of Okinawa, Mitscher's carrier provided cover from kamikazes approaching from Kyushu. Japanese air attacks proved light the first several days of the campaign but increased on April 6 when a force of 400 aircraft attempted to attack the fleet. The high point of the naval campaign came on April 7 when the Japanese launched **Operation Ten-Go**.

Operation Ten-Go (天號作戰 (Kyūjitai) or 天号作戦 (Shinjitai) Ten-gō Sakusen) was a Japanese naval operation plan in 1945

Operation Ten-Go - Background:

By early 1945, having suffered crippling defeats at the Battles of Midway, Philippine Sea, and Leyte Gulf, the Japanese Combined Fleet was reduced to a small number of operational warships. Concentrated in the home islands, these remaining vessels were too few in number to directly engage the Allies' fleets. As a final precursor to the invasion of Japan, Allied troops began attacking Okinawa on April 1, 1945. A month prior, realizing that Okinawa would be the Allies' next target, Emperor Hirohito convened a meeting to discuss plans for the island's defense.

Operation Ten-Go - The Japanese Plan:

Having listened to the army's plans to defend Okinawa through the use of kamikaze attacks and determined fighting on the ground, the Emperor demanded to how the navy planned to aid in the effort. Feeling pressured, the Commander in Chief of the Combined Fleet, Admiral Toyoda Soemu met with his planners and conceived Operation Ten-Go. A kamikaze-style operation, Ten-Go called for the massive battleship Yamato, the light cruiser Yahagi, and eight destroyers to fight their way through the Allied fleet and beach themselves on Okinawa.

Once ashore, the ships were to act as shore batteries until destroyed at which point their surviving crews were to disembark and fight as infantry. As the Navy's air arm had effectively been destroyed, no air cover would be available to support the effort. Though many, including the Ten-Go force commander Vice Admiral Seiichi Ito, felt that the operation was a waste of scant resources, Toyoda pushed it forward and preparations began. On March 29, Ito shifted his ships from Kure to Tokuyama. Arriving, Ito continued preparations but could not bring himself to order the operation to commence.

On April 5, Vice Admiral Ryunosuke Kusaka arrived in Tokuyama to convince the Combined Fleet's commanders to accept Ten-Go. Upon learning the details, most sided with Ito believing that the operation was a futile waste. Kusaka persisted and told them that the operation would draw American aircraft away from the army's planned air attacks on Okinawa and that the Emperor was expecting the navy to make a maximum effort in the island's defense. Unable to resist the Emperor's wishes, those in attendance reluctantly agreed to move forward with the operation.

Operation Ten-Go - The Japanese Sail:

Briefing his crews on the nature of the mission, Ito permitted any sailor who wished to stay behind to leave the ships (none did) and sent ashore new recruits, sick, and wounded. Through the day on April 6, intense damage-control drills were conducted and the ships fueled. Sailing at 4:00 PM, Yamato, and its consorts were spotted by the submarines USS Threadfin and USS Hackleback as they passed through the Bundo Strait. Unable to get into an attack position the submarines radioed in sighting reports. By dawn, Ito had cleared the Osumi Peninsula at the south end of Kyushu.

Shadowed by American reconnaissance aircraft, Ito's fleet was reduced on the morning of April 7 when the destroyer Asashimo developed engine trouble and turned back. At 10:00 AM, Ito feinted west in an attempt to make the Americans think he was retreating. After steaming west for an hour and a half, he returned to a southerly course after being spotted by two American PBY Catalinas. In an effort to drive off the aircraft, Yamato opened fire with its 18-inch guns using special "beehive" anti-aircraft shells.

Operation Ten-Go - The Americans Attack:

Aware of Ito's progress, the eleven carriers of Vice Admiral Marc Mitscher's Task Force 58 began launching several waves of aircraft around 10:00 AM. In addition, a force of six battleships and two large cruisers was sent north in case air strikes failed to stop the Japanese.

Flying north from Okinawa, the first wave spotted Yamato shortly after noon. As the Japanese lacked air cover, the American fighters, dive bombers, and torpedo planes patiently set up their attacks. Commencing around 12:30 PM, the torpedo bombers focused their attacks on Yamato's port side to increase the chances of the ship capsizing.

As the first wave struck, Yahagi was hit in the engine room by a torpedo. Dead in the water, the light cruiser was struck by six more torpedoes and twelve bombs in the course of the battle before sinking at 2:05 PM. While Yahagi was being crippled, Yamato took a torpedo and two bomb hits. Though not affecting its speed, a large fire erupted aft of the battleship's superstructure. The second and third waves of aircraft launched their attacks between 1:20 PM and 2:15 PM. maneuvering for its life; the battleship was hit by at least eight torpedoes and as many as fifteen bombs.

Losing power, Yamato began listing severely to port.

Due to the destruction of the ship's water damage-control station, the crew was unable to counter-flood specially designed spaces on the starboard side. At 1:33 PM, Ito ordered the starboard boiler and engine rooms flooded in an effort to right the ship. This effort killed the several hundred crewmen working in those spaces and reduced the ship's speed to ten knots. At 2:02 PM, Ito ordered the mission canceled and the crew to abandon ship. Three minutes later, Yamato began to capsize.

Around 2:20 PM, the battleship rolled completely and began to sink before being torn open by a massive explosion. Four of the Japanese destroyers were also sunk during the battle.

Operation Ten-Go - Aftermath:

Operation Ten-Go cost the Japanese between 3,700–4,250 dead as well as Yamato, Yahagi, and four destroyers. American losses were a mere twelve killed and ten aircraft. Operation Ten-Go was the Imperial Japanese Navy's last significant action of World War II and its few remaining ships would have little effect during the final weeks of the war. The operation had minimal effect on the Allied operations around Okinawa and the island was declared secure on June 21, 1945.

On April 1945, the Japanese battleship Yamato (the largest battleship in the world) along with nine other Japanese warships, embarked from Japan on a deliberate suicide attack upon Allied forces engaged in the Battle of Okinawa. The Japanese force was attacked, stopped, and almost destroyed by United States carrier-borne aircraft before reaching Okinawa. Yamato and five other Japanese warships were sunk.

They were attempting to run the battleship Yamato through the Allied fleet with the goal of beaching it on Okinawa for use a shore battery. Intercepted by Allied aircraft, Yamato and its escorts were immediately attacked. Struck by multiple waves of torpedo bombers and dive bombers from Mitscher's carriers, the battleship was sunk that afternoon.

As the land battle progressed, Allied naval vessels remained in the area and were subjected to a relentless succession of kamikaze attacks. Flying around 1,900 kamikaze missions, the Japanese sunk 36 Allied ships, mostly amphibious vessels, and destroyers. An additional 368 were damaged. As a result of these attacks, 4,907 sailors were killed and 4,874 were wounded. Due to the protracted and exhausting nature of the campaign, Nimitz took the drastic step of relieving his principal commanders at Okinawa to allow them to rest and recuperate. As result, Spruance was relieved by Admiral William Halsey in late May and Allied naval forces were re-designated the 3rd Fleet."

Leon Grabowsky joined the conversation and said, "The biggest problem with Okinawa was the lack of intel able to be retrieved. The kamikaze pilots planes were on fire and the burning flesh and smell of fuel – I'll never get that image out of my head. We had nothing to retrieve or nothing to move forward with upon conclusion of these attacks from the sea's perspective. Now let's talk about the finer details of, "**Operation Merchant.**"

Leon Grabowsky walked to the center of the room and said, "This mission will take courage. It will take everyone in this room; places where they have not gone before. We must not be afraid. Why do you think the Japanese kamikaze attacks are so successful?

Why? The answer is simple. It's because they are fearless. That's our new motivation – to be fearless. Do remember that your Blue Jacket code of conduct book – that means nothing to where we are going.

Below this deck, we have thirty Japanese soldiers with only twenty of them agreeing to our mission. Let's just say the other ten had a burning desire not to attend the mission. These twenty Jap's are now working for the US Navy. In a few moments; I'll be calling up Private First Class Henry Heinz. You see Henry as learned some Japanese very well and has been interacting with the captured soldiers. This skill will allow him to excel in our mission. This is most notable that most if not all Japanese soldiers would never turn against their country.

What is most important to know – these soldiers are vulnerable and scared. They are human beings like us and I'm ordering each and every one of you to treat them with the same respect you have for each other and me as your superiors. Do you understand?

"Yes Sir," was belted out my all of the Navy Sailors.

Leon Grabowsky continued explaining the mission.

Leon said, "Now that I have your attention; here is the mission we are to embark this time tomorrow. As we sit here in Norfolk – just outside you may have noticed a Japanese Merchant ship docked next to the DE-528. In a few moments, twenty of the Japs along with 50 of the 103rd Army Infantry and 300 of the 6th Armored Division will be brought on board to the DE-528 for a de-briefing by Henry Heinz. The Edogawa Maru (Kanji:江戸川丸) was a 6,968-ton Japanese transport ship that was sunk by USS Sunfish on 18 November 1944 with 2,114 lives lost.

This is what the Japanese had thought happened. The USS Sunfish was able to repair the ship and reclaim it in the hands of the US Navy. It's been here in Norfolk since the 02 December 1944.

Our mission is to use the Edogawa as bait for any passing Japanese to come aboard and assist. When they realize radio contact communication is down; they will send a unit to board. Visible will be ten Japanese me on the ships dock signaling them to board us. This is when we will ambush the partying crew but not until they are out of sight. The US army will capture and hold them hostage and when they notice their team has not come back; they will send more crew to us.

Depending on the ship; we could be faced with 400-1,000 men only a quarter of them a threat. Once we have captured; we will then seek Intel aboard the Japanese ship. We will look for ship deck logs and any Intel of where they have been and who they have been interacting with. Names and places will be crucial for our success. This is our mission and I'm your captain."

Chapter 10: Operation Dummy

December 31, 1945

Back at the *Sphere of the Holy Gate* – I'm wondering how I got so lucky to reconnect with my family. It seemed the phone call that was made to me occurred 5 years ago. I started to sort the letters and came across one of Tony's letter dated December 31, 1945. I said to Tony, "Let me read this one to everyone and you can tell us more about your experiences," John had said.

December 31, 1945

Dear Sis + Family,

Hope you are feeling fine as I am. Here I am in, Sick Bay again. Received your letter yesterday. You should be getting mine today. Yesterday, another kid and I took our boots off and went to the reception center. Alfred's father came to see him yesterday. We were also playing hide and go seek on a dry dock ship. We were the only 3 on board. The ship is only a dummy. That's where we got to sneak a smoke. I have to finish this letter standing up. There are about 200 guys that were in the sickbay. I am now sitting on the deck writing this letter. I'll close now with love and kisses. Special kisses to mom.

    - Tony

Tony said this letter is – well – a two-part story. Let me first start with sickbay. This is where I would sneak off and have time to write many letters to you and the family. You see many people were sick and it would give me time as I waited my turn to get many letters written from sickbay. I think Dr. Gill Miner figured out my plan as I was constantly in sickbay. I would call it Karma because a week before this letter was written I almost died. That is not a joke.

As we were traveling on our LCT freight ship we just had made a stop in the Philippines to pick up cargo and vehicles for land deployment. The Philippines mosquitos were a big problem and I had gotten eaten up a few days and consequently became ill. I had stopped and over to sick bay and spoke to the doctor about my symptoms.

We were losing many men due to disease and I was feared to become the next statistic. I looked at the doc and said, "I got the chills and fever and I feel miserable." The doctor who was optimistic about my hoax of a story. He must have seen through my deception before.

While shivering and clanking my teeth I looked over at the doc.

Doc, "I think I have malaria. It's become a problem and the mosquitos got to me." The doc had examined me and concluded on my condition.

Dr. Miner looked over at me. "You do in fact have a high temperature at 106 and malaria." As the news was delivered in haste I turned my head towards the rear of the quarters. The medical team had a section with a screen around it. I could see that many men were placed in this area to die.

I then turned back to the doctor and looked up at him.

"I'm going to win and beat this. I'm going to see another day on this ship. Then I'm going home to see my sis and family."

"Son, men have conquered malaria before," Dr. Miner said with a genuine smile. "And Men have also gone home to see their families."

As a day or two have passed, I felt much better and did, in fact, conquer malaria by letting my system fight it out. I was still weak and not in the proper mind for duty far from death.

Dr. Miner stopped by to check in on me. He did the usual checkup and could see a big improvement.

"I'm sorry Tony; we are greatly tight for room as you can tell. I know you aren't quite at 100 percent, but I'm going to release you later today."

I had accepted the fact of facing death and decided not to use the sick bay anymore for ways to write letters. This was an eye-opening experience and I realized I was selfish that people actually needed treatment.

The next story I'm about to tell you is not documented even to this day. It's called, "*Operation Dummy,*" and I was part of the crew who executed this operation.

As you had learned from my letter the US Navy would often have either decommissioned' chips or as what we refer to as – "Dummy Ships." These were used for training purposes and to practice drills before crews actually deployed into the sea. That was the main purpose but after *Operation Mincemeat* was successful the original intent of the dummy ships were changed.

Operation Mincemeat was a successful British disinformation strategy used in 1943 during the Allied invasion of Sicily. It comprised of two members of British intelligence obtained the body of Glyndwr Michael. He died from eating rat poison and was dressed as an officer of the Royal Marines and placed personal items on him identifying him as Captain William Martin. This allowed the finders of the body to follow planted evidence as a misdirection effort to know where they were going. This led to correspondence between two British generals which suggested invading Greece and Sardinia in 1943 instead of Sicily, the actual objective. This was accomplished by persuading the Germans that they had, by accident, intercepted "top secret" documents giving details of Allied war plans.

The documents were attached to a corpse deliberately left to wash up on a beach in Punta Umbría in Spain. The operation started with the planting of false documents but the use of the Enigma machine helped double agents working for the Allies. Our commanding officers also made by Operation Dummy on the premises of deception such as the Army's *Operation Fortitude South.*

Tony said to Pat, "You must know what Operation Fortitude South – is that a safe assumption?

Pat laughed and said, "Yes I'm aware of this operation dating back to 1943. Tony, do you mind if I tell the family about this operation?"

"Of course not – please do," Tony had said.

Pat signaled the group and said, "I think I have a photo of this to share with you. Huddle in."

Dummy Allied tank (Credit: Barcroft Media via Getty Images)

Pat began to tell the story as far as what was explained to him. D-Day was one of the largest land invasions in military history, but it was preceded by an equally elaborate campaign of subterfuge known as Operation Fortitude South. Spearheaded by the British, Fortitude South was a ruse designed to deceive the Germans into thinking the Allies would make landfall in France at the Pas de Calais instead of Normandy. To help sell the con, the Allies created a fictitious invasion force known as the "First U.S. Army Group" and fed the Germans phony intelligence suggesting the phantom army would lead a charge on the Pas de Calais.

Operatives used inflatable tanks, wooden airplanes and dummy fuel depots to trick reconnaissance pilots into believing that the First U.S. Army Group was assembled in Kent, England—the most likely staging ground for an attack on the Pas de Calais. To top it all off, they even placed the much-feared General George Patton in charge of the fake army to lend it an additional air of authenticity.

Operation Fortitude South continued even after the Allies launched their invasion of Normandy on June 6, 1944. Aircraft focused many of their bombings runs on the Pas de Calais instead of Normandy, and double agents worked to convince the Germans that the D-Day invasion was merely a feint designed to screen a second, larger offensive from the south. The swarm of contradictory reports, bluffs and misdirects ultimately had their intended effect. When the Allies stormed the beaches at Normandy, the Germans had a large concentration of troops languishing at the Pas de Calais, waiting for an assault that never came.

In the same manner, "Operation Dummy," was executed based on these premises of misdirection of both of these concepts and I'll explain what the intent was with this operation.

I was onboard LCS(L)-119 and the dummy ship that I mentioned in the letter was an identical match of the LCS-119 which was used on May 29th, 1945 for *Operation Dummy*. I was aboard the Dummy ship en-route to meet up with DD-741, real LCS-119 and LSD-30 off of Okinawa.

Just a day before May 29th on May 28th Off Okinawa we had suffered many kamikazes attacks which sank destroyer Drexler (DD-741) and damaged the attack transport Sandoval (APA-194). Within the Pacific, we also had the large support landing craft LCS(L)-119.

The sky was full of kamikaze Japanese Planes which tried to act as suicide missions and damage our ships. Around 1600 and for the next few hours an intense attack was underway on May 28th, 1945. We came close to another suicide crash into the LSD-30 off Okinawa. However, the ships laid gunfire and managed to deflect the Japanese plane from its suicidal course toward the amidships deckhouse and into a less vulnerable part. These actions resulted in saving the ship from worse damage. There are no fatalities on board but led us to execute *Operation Dummy*. Our Captain Leon Grabowsky just had us execute *Operation Merchant* in April and that's another story to tell. He was a smart intelligent man who was ahead of our times. Under his command, we always seemed to have an edge against our enemy. When all said and done the raid on the Pacific the Japanese had used over 1900 planes and sank 26 USA ships.

Our ship was at sea for 5 days and while our Captain Leon Grabowsky had ordered one of our CPO's (Chief Petty Officer) to learn Japanese while we were at sea.

We had arrived just shortly after the intense battle had subsided and we had pulled next to LSD-30 and the real LCS-119 in our dummy LCS-119. The ship LSD-30 was being put out as it was on fire and alongside the ship contained much debris from airplanes and sunken airplanes. As we approached within close proximity we had received a call from the real LCS-119. They had let us know to anchor within 20 meters of our location and take a small boat onto the LSD-30. The had told us the US Navy divers were retrieving radio's, documents, and uniforms from the wreckage of the planes.

This initiative was part of *Operation Dummy*.

Annie had interrupted me.

"What was your role in Operation Dummy," she had said. Glad you asked Tony had said and pulled us back into the Story.

The captain assembled a few of us to board a small rescue boat so we wouldn't interfere with the divers across the way. While we boarded a small boat it was a horrific scene. The smell of burning plane fuel and the stench in the air was enough to almost make you pass out due to the toxic fumes in the air. As we were traveling towards the LSD-30 to inquire on repairs I noticed several divers who were coming out of cockpits of planes that were half submerged but didn't quite go under yet. I saw a diver pull some documents off one of the deceased Imperial Japanese Airforce men. It appeared to be some type of protocol book.

He was also preparing the deceased body to be carried away. I thought to myself what are we up too? We finally arrived and boarded the LSD-30 which was on fire while the crew was spraying it down with water. It was my job to inspect and repair the communications as it took a hit for the worse during the kamikaze attack. Before – I was left alone to work on this task the Captain wanted to brief us on the other task at hand called, *"Operation Dummy."*

Captain Grabowsky gathered the crew for a quick formal meeting.

[He proposed his speech to the crew]

You are back standing with me once again. Just a month previously each and every one of you helped with – Operation Merchant which was successful as planned. We meet in a similar situation once again and in order to be successful, we must work together again. As you have noticed during the short ride up on our small craft the navy divers were retrieving items from shot down Japanese airplanes.

Now, most what's in the sea was modified Japanese airplanes. You see airplanes intended for Kamikaze attacks were typically stripped from machine guns, bombs, and communication radios which allowed bigger gas tanks to be used. For the fighter planes being used to fight deemed different findings. Findings in which you would typically assume would be on such aircrafts such as machine guns, bombs, and communications. We got lucky guys.

[As Captain Grabowsky is explaining; the divers had arrived to brief the captain on their findings]

The divers arrived and asked permission to speak freely. The captain had agreed.

We found one particular aircraft that had communications as well as distress documents along with the uniform in a quite good shape with no holes, blood, and etc.

[The divers had handed the Captain the uniform and distress documents]

Captain then continued to brief the crew on the mission.

In my hands, I hold the key ingredients for Operation Dummy. Before explaining these items; I would like to call up Henry Heinz who most of you know. He has been learning Japanese for many months in preparation of this Operation. The Wabun code (和文モールス符号 wabun mōrusu fugō, Japanese text in Morse code) is a form of Morse code used to send Japanese text. Unlike the International Morse Code, which represents letters of the Latin script, in Wabun each symbol represents a Japanese kana. For this reason, Wabun code is also sometimes called Kana code.

When Wabun Code is intermixed with International Morse code, the prosign DO (-..---) is used to announce the beginning of Wabun, and the prosign SN (...-.) is used to return to International Code. Let me explain the mission scope in detailed order along with the roles and responsibilities of each crew member. I will read the "Official" memorandum approved by Fleet Admiral Ernest King on May 1, 1945. Once finished reading the letter Henry Heinz will brief us on what his specific role will be during this operation.

[Leon begins to read the letter to the crew]

Confidential – Operation Dummy
Us Navy Pacific Fleet
Approved by Fleet Admiral Ernest J. King
Executed by Captain Leon Grabowky
Approved Date: February 1, 1945
Operation Date: May 20, 1945

Purpose: To lure the Japanese fleet in the proximity of Bandjermasin, Indonesia by deception. Japanese vessels that enter this area will be destroyed by Submarine Blenny (SS-324) while operating in conjunction with Project Rainbow.

Operational Outline:
1. **Train seaman to learn the Japanese Language prior to mission go-live of May 20, 1945**
2. **Stage dummy ship LCS-119 Approximately 50 miles from Bandjermasin, Indonesia in the Jawa Sea. Onboard will be Henry Heinz**

3. Before May 20th; we will need to retrieve Japanese Imperial Uniforms, Radio Transmitter, and official distress communication protocol used by the Japanese.

4. The DD-741 will use cloaking devices to appear invisible as per Project Rainbow. Alongside the DD-741 will be the SS-324 in preparation to strike and will also be cloaked.

5. On March 20, 1945, a distress signal will be sent using the Wabun code by Henry Heinz to lure the Japanese fleet to his location aboard the LCS-119.

6. Named Seaman bearing the Japanese Language will indicate he captured the LCS-119 and crashed his plane nearby.

7. Once the Japanese fleet comes visible the SS-324 will submerge and fire when in range of 9,000 yards at 8 knots operating speed.

8. Once successful the US Pacific Fleet will overtake the vessel and move in with the DD-741 and LCS-119 alongside the SS-324.

9. Once captured the US Pacific Fleet will capture any crew members and surrender all documents to the C/O.

Leon said, "Does anyone have any concerns or questions on what we must do at this time?"

Chapter 11: Battle of Anzio
December 31, 1945

"Pass the box over to me Vic," Pat had said.

Oh yes – this is an important battle. Let me tell you about the Battle of Anzio. The Battle of Anzio was a battle of the Italian Campaign of World War II that took place from January 22, 1944–with the Allied amphibious landing known as Operation Shingle–to June 5, 1944, with the capture of Rome. The operation was opposed by German forces in the area of Anzio and Nettuno.

Operation Shingle was originally conceived by British Prime Minister Winston Churchill in December 1943, as he lay recovering from pneumonia in Marrakesh. His concept was to land two divisions at Anzio, bypassing German forces in central Italy, and take Rome, the strategic objective of the current Battle of Rome. By January he had recovered and was badgering his commanders for a plan of attack, accusing them of not wanting to fight but of being interested only in drawing pay and eating rations. General Harold Alexander, commander of the Allied Armies in Italy, had already considered such a plan since October using five divisions. However, the 5th Army did not have the troops or the means to transport them. Clark proposed landing a reinforced division to divert German troops from Monte Cassino. This second landing, however, instead of failing similarly, would hold "the shingle" for a week in expectation of a breakthrough at Cassino, and so the operation was named Shingle.

The Anzio beachhead is at the northwestern end of a tract of reclaimed marshland, formerly the Pontine Marshes, now the Pontine Fields (Agro Pontino). Previously uninhabitable due to mosquitoes carrying malaria, in Roman time's armies marched as quickly as possible across it on the military road, the Via Appia. The marsh was bounded on one side by the sea and on others by mountains: the Monti Albani, the Monti Lepini, the Monti Ausoni and further south the Monti Aurunci (where the allies had been brought to a halt before Monte Cassino).

Overall these mountains are referenced by the name Monti Laziali, the mountains of Lazio, the ancient Latium. Invading armies from the south had the choice of crossing the marsh or taking the only other road to Rome, the Via Latina, running along the eastern flanks of the Monti Laziali, risking entrapment. The marshes were turned into cultivatable land in the 1930s under Benito Mussolini. Canals and pumping stations were built to remove the brackish water from the land. These canals divided the land into personal tracts with new stone houses for colonists from north Italy. Mussolini also founded the five cities destroyed by the battle.

When Lucian Truscott's 3rd Division was first selected for the operation, he pointed out to Clark that the position was a death trap and there would be no survivors. Agreeing, Clark canceled the operation, but Prime Minister Churchill revived it. Apparently, the two allies had different concepts: the Americans viewed such a landing as another distraction from Cassino, but if they could not break through at Cassino, the men at Anzio would be trapped. Churchill and the British high command envisioned an outflanking movement ending with the capture of Rome. Mediterranean Theatre commander General Dwight D. Eisenhower, leaving to take command of Operation

Overlord left the decision up to Churchill with a warning about German unpredictability. Both sides finally agreed that the troops could not remain at Anzio, but Lucas received somewhat equivocal orders.

He was to lead the Fifth Army's U.S. VI Corps in a surprise landing in the Anzio area, and make a rapid advance into the Alban Hills to cut German communications and "threaten the rear of the German XIV Panzer Corps" under General Fridolin von Senger und Etterlin. It was hoped that this threat would draw Germany's forces away from the Cassino area and facilitate an Allied breakthrough there. No one saw the point of taking the Alban Hills, nor was Churchill's idea of a flanking movement expressed.

Planners argued that if Kesselring (in charge of German forces in Italy) pulled troops out of the Gustav Line to defend against the Allied assault, then Allied forces would be able to break through the line; if Kesselring didn't pull troops out of the Gustav Line, then Operation Shingle would threaten to capture Rome and cut off the German units defending the Gustav Line. Should Germany have adequate reinforcements available to defend both Rome and the Gustav Line, the Allies felt that the operation would nevertheless be useful in engaging forces which could otherwise be committed on another front. The operation was officially canceled on December 18, 1943. However, it was later reselected.

Clark did not feel he had the numbers on the southern front to exploit any breakthrough. His plan, therefore, was relying on the southern offensive drawing Kesselring's reserves in and providing the Anzio force the opportunity to break inland quickly. This would also reflect the orders he had received from Alexander to "carry out an assault landing on the beaches in the vicinity of Rome with the object of cutting the enemy lines of communication and threatening the rear of the German XIV Corps [on the Gustav Line]." However, his written orders to Lucas did not really reflect this. Initially, Lucas had received orders to

1. Seize and secure a beachhead in the vicinity of Anzio

2. Advance and secure Colli Laziali [the Alban Hills]

3. Be prepared to advance on Rome".

However, Clark's final orders stated: "Advance on Colli Laziali" giving Lucas considerable flexibility as to the timing of any advance on the Alban Hills. It is likely that the caution displayed by both Clark and Lucas was to some extent a product of Clark's experiences at the tough battle for the Salerno beachhead and Lucas' natural caution stemming from his lack of experience in battle.

Neither Clark nor Lucas had full confidence in either their superiors or the operational plan. Along with most of the Fifth Army staff, they felt that Shingle was properly a two corps or even a full army task. A few days prior to the attack, Lucas wrote in his diary, "They will end up putting me ashore with inadequate forces and get me in a serious jam... Then, who will get the blame? [The operation] has a strong odor of Gallipoli and apparently, the same amateur was still on the coach's bench." The "amateur" can only have referred to Winston Churchill, architect of the disastrous Gallipoli landings of World War I and personal advocate of Shingle.

One of the problems with the plan was the availability of landing ships. The American commanders, in particular, were determined that nothing should delay the Normandy invasion and the supporting landings in southern France. Operation Shingle would require the use of landing ships necessary for these operations.

Initially, Shingle was to release these assets by January 15. However, this being deemed problematic, President Roosevelt granted permission for the craft to remain until February 5.

Only enough tank landing ships (LSTs) to land a single division were initially available to Shingle. Later, at Churchill's personal insistence, enough were made available to land two divisions. Allied intelligence thought that five or six German divisions were in the area, although U.S. 5th Army intelligence severely underestimated the German 10th Army's fighting capacity at the time, believing many of their units would be worn out after the defensive battles fought since September.

The LCT's of the navy would carry Army Forces to strategic locations. I'm surprised I wasn't carried to the location by Vic or John as that would be pretty comical to reunite with my brothers.

Allied forces in this attack consisted of 5 cruisers, 24 destroyers, 238 landing craft, 62+ other ships, 40,000 soldiers, and 5,000+ vehicles.

The attack consisted of three groups:

1. **The British force ("Peter Beach")** - This force attacked the coast 6 miles (9.7 km) north of Anzio
2. **The northwestern U.S. Force ("Yellow Beach")** - This force attacked the port of Anzio.

3. **The southwestern U.S. Force ("X-Ray Beach")-** This force attacked the coast east of Nettuno: 6 miles (9.7 km) east of Anzio. The invasion plan originally assigned the 504th Parachute Infantry Regiment to make a parachute assault near Aprilia, eight miles north of Anzio, which would have placed it in position for an early capture of the key road junction at Campoleone, which was not taken until late May. However, these plans were scrapped on 20 January, apparently because of the high losses during the airborne assaults at Sicily. The 504th PIR was then assigned to land by the sea.

4. **Southern attack-** The Fifth Army's attack on the Gustav Line began on January 16, 1944, at Monte Cassino. Although the operation failed to break through, it did succeed in part in its primary objective. Heinrich von Vietinghoff, commanding the Gustav Line, called for reinforcements, and Kesselring transferred the 29th and 90th Panzergrenadier Divisions from Rome.

I was part of the "Southern Attack," and will read some letters dated in May of 1944 which was an interesting few months on the front line.

At 5:45 a.m. May 23, 1944, 1,500 Allied artillery pieces commenced bombardment. Forty minutes later the guns paused as attacks were made by close air support and then resumed as the infantry moved forward. The first day's fighting was intense: the 1st Armored Division lost 100 tanks and 3rd Infantry Division suffered 955 casualties, the highest single-day figure for any U.S. division during World War II. The Germans suffered too, with the 362nd Infantry Division estimated to have lost 50% of its fighting strength

Men of 'D' Company, 1st Battalion, Green Howards, part of 15th Brigade of British 5th Division, occupy a captured German communications trench during the breakout at Anzio, Italy, 22 May 1944.

Mackensen had been convinced that the Allies' main thrust would be up to the Via Anziate, and the ferocity of the British feint on May 23 and 24 did nothing to persuade him otherwise. Kesselring, however, was convinced that the Allies' intentions were to gain Route 6 and ordered the Hermann Göring Panzer Division, resting 150 miles (240 km) away at Livorno, to Valmontone to hold open Route 6 for the Tenth Army, which was retreating up this road from Cassino.

In the afternoon of May 25, Cisterna finally fell to 3rd Division who had had to go house to house winkling out the German 362nd Infantry which had refused to withdraw and, as a consequence, had virtually ceased to exist by the end of the day. By the end of May 25, 3rd Infantry was heading into the Velletri gap near Cori, and elements of 1st Armored had reached within 3 miles (4.8 km) of Valmontone and were in contact with units of the Herman Göring Division which were just starting to arrive from Leghorn.[nb 1] Although VI Corps had suffered over 3,300 casualties in the three days fighting, Operation Buffalo was going to plan, and Truscott was confident that a concerted attack by 1st Armored and 3rd Infantry Divisions the next day would get his troops astride Route 6.

Then the final move on Rome.

On the evening of May 25, Truscott received new orders from Clark via his Operations Officer, Brigadier General Don Brand. These were, in effect, to implement Operation Turtle and turn the main line of attack 90 degrees to the left. Most importantly, although the attack towards Valmontone and Route 6 would continue, 1st Armored was to withdraw to prepare to exploit the planned breakthrough along the new line of attack leaving 3rd Division to continue towards Valmontone with 1st Special Service Force in support. Clark informed Alexander of these developments late in the morning of May 26 by which time the change of orders was a fait accompli. At the time, Truscott was shocked, writing later "I was dumbfounded. This was no time to drive to the north-west where the enemy was still strong; we should pour our maximum power into the Valmontone Gap to ensure the destruction of the retreating German Army. I would not comply with the order without first talking to General Clark in person.

However, he was not on the beachhead and could not be reached even by radio.... such as the order that turned the main effort of the beachhead forces from the Valmontone Gap and prevented the destruction of the German Tenth Army. On the 26th the order was put into effect." He went on to write "There has never been any doubt in my mind that had General Clark held loyally to General Alexander's instructions, had he not changed the direction of my attack to the north-west on May 26, the strategic objectives of Anzio would have been accomplished in full. To be first in Rome was a poor compensation for this lost opportunity".

On May 26, while the VI Corps was initiating its difficult maneuver, Kesselring threw elements of four divisions into the Velletri gap to stall the advance on Route 6. For four days they slugged it out against 3rd Division until finally withdrawing on May 30, having kept Route 6 open and allowed seven divisions from 10th Army to withdraw and head north of Rome.

On the new axis of attack, little progress was made until 1st Armored were in position on May 29, when the front advanced to the main Caesar C Line defenses. Nevertheless, an early breakthrough seemed unlikely until on May 30 Major General Fred Walker's 36th Division found a gap in the Caesar Line at the join between 1st Parachute Corps and LXXVI Panzer Corps. Climbing the steep slopes of Monte Artemisio they threatened Velletri from the rear and obliged the defenders to withdraw. This was a key turning point, and von Mackensen offered his resignation which Kesselring accepted.

Raising the pressure further, Clark assigned U.S. II Corps which, fighting its way along the coast from the Gustav Line had joined up with VI Corps on May 25 to attack around the right-hand side of the Alban Hills and advance along the line of Route 6 to Rome.

On June 2 the Caesar Line collapsed under the mounting pressure, and 14th Army commenced a fighting withdrawal through Rome. On the same day Hitler, fearing another Battle of Stalingrad, had ordered Kesslering that there should be "no defense of Rome". Over the next day, the rearguards were gradually overwhelmed, and Rome was entered in the early hours of June 4 with Clark holding an impromptu press conference on the steps of the Town Hall on the Capitoline Hill that morning. He ensured the event was a strictly American affair by stationing military police at road junctions to refuse entry to the city by British military personnel.

Pat had looked at everyone and saw all of the faces – faces of relief of what could have been. Pat had said, "As you can see this was quite the battle and I made it. My first letter is dated March 10, 1944, and the second is May 6, 1944.

March 10, 1944
ANZIO

Dear Sis (Rose),

Just a few lines to let you know I'm in the best of health, and am always thinking of you. I guess all my back has finally caught up to me. Tonight at mail call, I received five letters. Four from you and a 3 sheet V-mail from our sis. About six days ago I received 48 letters. Most of them were from you and sis and I heard from quite a few of my friends. They were all addressed to the "5th Guards." About four days I received 19 letters addressed to the same and a couple of days ago I received 24 letters. Think of how my pen point is going to look when I get through writing to all of these people. In the past few weeks, I've received over 100 letters. Solid, eh! I'll have writer's cramp before I get through answering them. Sis you asked me why I wasn't going to write so often. Well, it's not because I'll be moving. From now on I'll see if I can get out a letter a day to you and sis. Because U know how one can feel when he doesn't get the mail. Very sorry to hear about Ann's trouble. I hope she and Frank take it all night. Give them by best will you sis? So mom goes downtown from Wethersfield Ave eh! Well, you tell her she won't have to ride the buses when I get back because she's been riding my new 1940 "Buick," which I will buy shortly after the war. I bet you think I'm kidding. Well, sis, with all the mail I have to catch up on. Love and Kisses
You're Kid Brother
Pat

May 6, 1944
ANZIO

Dear Sis,

I want you to know, I am a very happy man. Between yesterday and today, I've received over 50 letters. When was it about 8 days ago, I was mad as good because I wasn't getting mail, and now I got a big batch of them? Keep up the good work sis for that's all I came for here is the mail. How about sending me another picture because I'm going to send this one back to Lump's. I know he wants it as bad as I do, so please send me one. Believe it or not, I told the fellows that I couldn't recognize whether that was you or sis (rose). After looking at it a while, I see it's you. At times you two look just alike. Our rations came in today and this time it cost me 30 cents for 5 bars of candy, 2 Babe Ruth's, 1 Mounds, 2 Butterfingers, bar of Lux soap and a wick, plus a flint for my cigarette lighter. Most of the fellows who were here with this outfit since it invaded North Africa are now starting to go home on the rotating list. In exactly 4 days most of them will be overseas 2 full years. This is the outfit that did most of the fighting in North Africa with me. It's a good thing we were an armored division just think the poor guys who have to stay up the front lines for a week and maybe months without getting relieved. We go to the front lines but not as often as other divisions and only for short period of times. God Bless and Kisses to All – Your Kid Brother Pat

Chapter 12: Drug the Captain
December 31, 1945

Back at the Sphere of the Holy Gate we learn about John Lombardo's story.

John said to the group, "You're going to love my story. Let me tell you about drugging the captain. Pass the box." One of the navy sailors had asked to see me near the engine room.

Navy Sailor Neal said, "Can you believe this Captain? Didn't you hear?"

John said, "No – hear what? And who are you again?"

Navy Sailor Neal, "My name is Neal, F 2/C Pipefitter. We've had chow a few times, do you remember?"

John smacked his head and said, "Oh right, Neal. How are you?"

Neal exhaled and said, "I'm well for now. I was washing laundry with the cook. The cook is told by the Captain that he needs some chow. So the cook rushes and accidentally put the blues with the white's and ruined the clothes. I got in trouble with my inspection being my clothes were out of place and took the fall. Can you believe it the captain is hungry and demands a meal right there and then? "

John responded and said, "That's not right but after all don't you think he has earned the respect to do that."

Neal with a convincing tone in his voice said, "Don't worry I have something planned."

John with a look of concern had said, "What do you mean?"

Neal in a soft voice said, "I'm going to drug the captain. The cook feels bad for what happened and agreed to help me. I've seen the doctor and got some pills."

John was disgusted. "You can't be serious. Over laundry," John had said.

Neal had said, "It cost me a liberty. You know I'm only 22 years old and my freedom is everything. I'm honored to fight for this country but if you take my only free time away just because you want to eat food – I'm not ok with that John."

John was backing up on the way outside of the corridor and said, "I want no part of this. You hear me – no part."

In that moment; we were now back in the, "*Sphere of the Holy Gate*," well only for a moment. Before saying goodbye and reflecting on this story and all of the stories – a big white light carried uneasy over my eyes.

I had awakened back at the Oak Trees in Hartford, Connecticut alongside with Tony. Our bodies were pressed up against the trees outside from public view.

John to Tony, "Wow; it was a good experience. We just witnessed a real-life history lesson from our own walking blood."

Tony said, "I know everyone looked so energetic. I'd kill to be back in that time. I'm a walking dead weight now."

John laughed and said, "Oh come on. You look good. Let's go see Annie now."

We had come through the forest and made it back into the reception of the Evergreen Hospice facility.

Chapter 13: Remembering Annie
May 2007

Back at the Evergreen Hospice Facility in Hartford, Conn.

Nurse Clifford had arrived to provide Annie her medication dose for the day. Annie, "It's time for your meds," said Nurse Clifford as she entered the room.

Once again, "Annie; it's time for your meds," said Nurse Clifford. Annie was in the room in a rocking chair facing the window but had yet to respond to the Nurse's verbal commands. The nurse had approached Annie closer. She had found a DVD, "Letters for Iwo Jima," on the floor and her eyes were closed.

The nurse began to check her vitals and determined she had passed away. She approached the telephone and followed protocol to notify the internal staff and next of kin as well as the funeral home.

Meanwhile, Tony and John were on their way into the hospice facility at the moment and had approached the manager who previously checked them in earlier in the day.

John said, "We are here to see Annie Connerton."

Hospice Manager asked, "Are you, family?"

John replied, "Yes that's right."

The Hospice Manager responded with deep sorrow in his voice and said, "I'm sorry to say, Annie has passed away and arrangements are being made with the funeral home."

John started laughing and Tony followed suit. Hospice Manager looked confused and said, "Sir are You ok."

John said, "Yeah I'm fine."

Hospice Manager said, "Do we need to call anyone."

John said, "I'm sorry but Annie is not dead she is alive. I can't explain it but know God is watching over her. Thanks."

Hospice Manager said, "You're welcome."

In the next few days; I had re-visited the grave sites of Annie, John, and Vic in Connecticut to wish them a few words. I find it very therapeutic to talk to your loved one' and believe somehow they can hear me.

John had stopped over the graves in Connecticut and said, "Boys everything you have endured; I'm so proud of you. It was good seeing you in, "The Sphere of the Holy Gate."

John said to John, "I can't eat a pound of spaghetti in 2 minutes." I had walked up to the grave site of my father Vic and stopped and looked down.

John said to Vic, "Dad; I'm still learning how to play the drums. I'm almost as good as you were. I won't let you down. I'm going to see Annie next. Can you believe we are writing a book about Annie and the Letters?"

Upon leaving I had tapped on the headstone of the Lombardo's as a sign of good luck and friendship. I do hope one day they are able to hear me and connect with me. Just on the other side of the graveyard was Annie's grave.

I had kneeled down in front of Annie's grave with rosemary beads in my hand.

John said, "Dear Annie. Annie...Annie...Annie. It was good seeing you in the, "Sphere of the Holy Gate. Can you believe we are writing a book about you and the letters?"

I started to laugh and cry at the same time. When you have such emotions tied into your experience with Annie and the boys, I guess it's ok to have mixed emotion I had thought. I shrugged it off. At that moment; I had felt something touch my left shoulder. What was this I wondered? Was it one of the boys? Was it Annie? My heart was racing. I started to look around. I stood up but could not see anything. Was my earlier suspicion correct? Maybe somehow they could hear me.

My eyes started to wander – back and forth. As I looked around for anything; all I saw were flowers and grave stone's end to end on this bright sunny day. I had wondered; was I that emotionally and perhaps maybe I'm hallucinating.

As my eyes had come to my 2 o'clock position I had noticed a glow coming from behind one of the trees. I waited for a few moments and then my mouth dropped to the floor. At that moment; a young Annie emerged from behind the tree line. It was the same Annie from, "*The Sphere of the Holy Gate.*"

She was in my line of sight approximately 40-50 feet from me. We had both noticed each other and she waved her hand without any verbal commands. She then turned away and started to walk at an accelerated speed down the grass way between the other gravestones.

I had immediately leaped into motion. I started to follow and ran towards her with the Rosemary Beads in hand. I started to yell her name. As I came closer within 8-10 feet she had vanished in front of my eyes. She was gone. This was the last time I saw Annie Connerton.

Conclusion

World War II was the deadliest military conflict in history. An estimated total of 70-85 million people perished, which was about 3% of the 1940 world population (est. 2.3 billion). The story of the Lombardo brothers has opened up my eyes to unravel the challenges of war. It was not just a battle against the enemy. As you have read in this book; the brothers had conquered over diseases, weather, conflict with others, and so much more. In order to have a level of sanity letters were sent back in exchange to tell the tempo and things on the minds of each Lombardo.

As seen in the film and this book; these young men who served in WW2 never knew if they were writing their last letters to loved ones. The Lombardo's were thankful to survive the war but some were not. Most of the men have never lived independently and had to be responsible for themselves. While wondering when the war will end could most certainly put a burden on one's mind?

However some men did, in fact, write their own letters – the last letter and words to be seen. As an example; Private Harry Schiraldi was a medic from New York and served with the 116th Infantry Regiment, 29th Infantry Division. He was stationed at Omaha Beach, Normandy, which was "littered with dead and wounded troops, and the tide brings in dead men,"

Excerpt from the letter on May 31, 1944

"Dear Ma, Just a few lines tonight to let you know that I'm fine and hope everybody at home is in the best of health. I just finished playing baseball and took a nice shower and now I feel very nice.

Hope everything is going alright at home and don't forget if you ever need money you could cash my war bonds anything you want to. This afternoon I went to church and I received Holy Communion again today. Getting holy, isn't I? Well, Ma, that's all I got to say tonight so I'll close with my love to all and hope to hear from you very soon. Take care of yourself. One of your loving sons, Harry"

A response was sent to the family with this message dated on July 18 that he had been missing since the 6th of June which was just eighteen days later.

"THE SECRETARY OF WAR DESIRES ME TO EXPRESS HIS DEEP REGRET THAT YOUR SON PRIVATE HARRY SCHIRALDI HAS BEEN REPORTED MISSING IN ACTION SINCE SIX JUNE IN FRANCE IF FURTHER DETAILS OR OTHER INFORMATION ARE RECEIVED YOU WILL BE PROMPTLY NOTIFIED."

Harry did, in fact, write his last letter. This reminded me of how much Annie worried if she would have heard the bad news. Or perhaps letters would just stop coming into her. The stress between being on the front lines or out in the Ocean with not knowing what today or tomorrow would bring must have been overwhelming for everyone.

I have also wondered what additional responsibilities the Lombardo's might have been ordered to do. With Malaria and diseases did certain duties get merged among the crew's responsibilities? I had wondered being in a war on a battleship with the sound of explosions and US Navy crew injured when would you have to step up and do someone else's job. I'm sure something like this occurred where the Lombardo's were ordered to take on additional work and or in the heat of the movement had to volunteer to take over a role that was foreign to them for the sake of survival.

This reminded me of a story dating back to 1941. On the morning of Sunday, Dec. 7, 1941, West Virginia was moored at a berth along Pearl Harbor's Battleship Row. Shortly after 8 a.m., although the two countries were at peace, waves of Japanese carrier-borne aircraft swooped in over Oahu and within minutes of the first wave,

Miller's ship was hit by at least six torpedoes and two bombs, sparking fires that would last 30 hours, leave the ship on the bottom of the harbor, and at least 106 members of her crew dead.

Texan Doris "Dorie" Miller did not let the fact that he wasn't trained on a machine gun to stop him when he saw Japanese aircraft come in low over Pearl Harbor. Doris primary function was the US Navy's and never fired or used this weapon before. The cook, who had not been trained to use the gun, then manned one of the ship's nine water-cooled .50 caliber Browning anti-aircraft machine guns until it ran dry and he was ordered to abandon ship.

Miller described firing the machine gun during the battle, a weapon which he had not been trained to operate: "It wasn't hard. I just pulled the trigger and she worked fine. I had watched the others with these guns. I guess I fired her for about fifteen minutes. I think I got one of those Jap planes. They were diving pretty close to us."

Five months later, Miller was personally presented with the Navy Cross by Adm. Nimitz aboard the carrier Enterprise, the first African-American to receive the Navy's second-highest decoration awarded for valor in combat.

I want to take a moment to recognize the Vic, John, Pat, and Tony for their courage during WW2. This book is dedicated to the entire Lombardo Family.

- I would also like to thank all active serving military personnel and those who served this fine country. Those who lost their life's serving – we salute you.

Joseph McGee

In Memory

Vic Lombardo: He served in the US Navy as Machinery Repairmen & Radio Electrician. He spent most of his service time in the South Pacific Ocean. He attended US Navy Training School for (RADIO) for Company Five in 1944.

1926 - 1979

John Lombardo: John Lombardo served in the US Navy as Machinery Repairmen & Machinist's Mate in 1941. He was part of the Sub Group 3 "M" Division and associated with the USS Demeter (ARB-10). Once discharged, John had many jobs until he joined the West Hartford Post Office for a term over 30 years.

1921 – 1988

In Memory

Tony Lombardo: He served in the US Navy as Machinery Repairmen in 1945 for the US Navy. Tony served his country honorably with the US Navy during World War II. Prior to retiring many years ago, he was a mail carrier for the East Hartford, CT Postal Service for 30 years.

1928 - 2011

Pat Lombardo: He served in the US Army in 1943 during World War II, serving with the 1st Armored Division, Fifth Army, and 6th Armored Division in Italy and Africa. Pat was awarded two Bronze Stars for bravery. He was proud to have been chosen to be a personal guard to General Eisenhower. Pat worked in the East Hartford Post Office until he retired in 1984.

1923 - 2005

Annie Connerton

1919- 2017

Picture Gallery

Vic Lombardo

Vic Lombardo

Annie Connerton

Pat Lombardo

John Lombardo

Tony Lombardo

Left- Vic Lombardo

Lombardo Group Photo

Annie and Tony Lombardo

Annie Connerton

Tony Lombardo

Pat Lombardo

Pat, Patricia, Annie, and Jim

Pat Lombardo – Fifth Army

Annie on the Drums...

Pat and Patricia

Pat and Patricia

Pat Lombardo's Bronze Star Medal- 1945

Pat Lombardo (left) with 1st Infantry Division

Tony Lombardo – Wedding

Vic Lombardo

Glossary

Fictious Events Created by the Author

The Sphere of the Holy Gate – A fictitious place created by the author as the sphere to heaven. Chapter 2.

Operation Merchant- A fictious operation created by the author. This Operation was to capture a Merchant Japanese Vessel for Intel.

Operation Dummy- A fictious operation created by the author. The US Navy did use "Dummy" ships for training but there was no such operation code named for it. This operation was to deflect radar with new sonar deflection tactics. Project Rainbow inspired this event. The "Philadelphia Experiment" was an alleged naval military experiment at the Philadelphia Naval Shipyard in Philadelphia, Pennsylvania, sometime around 28 October 1943, in which Eldridge was to be rendered invisible (i.e. by a cloaking device) to human observers for a brief period. It is also referred to as Project Rainbow.

Real Events

Operation Raincoat-The Battle for Monte La Difensa, which took place between 3 December and 9 December 1943, occurred during Operation Raincoat, part of the Battle for the Bernhardt Line during the Italian Campaign in World War II.

Operation Encore- The Battle of Monte Castello (also called Operation Encore) was an engagement which took place from 25 November 1944 to 21 February 1945 during the Italian campaign of World War II. It was fought between the Allied forces advancing into northern Italy and dug-in German defenders.

Operation Mincemeat- Operation Mincemeat was a successful British deception of the Second World War to disguise the 1943 Allied invasion of Sicily. Two members of British intelligence obtained the body of Glyndwr Michael, a tramp who died from eating rat poison, dressed him as an officer of the Royal Marines and placed personal items on him identifying him as the fictitious Captain (Acting Major) William Martin. Correspondence between two British generals which suggested that the Allies planned to invade Greece and Sardinia, with Sicily as merely the target of a feint, was also placed on the body.

Port Chicago Disaster- The Port Chicago disaster was a deadly munitions explosion that occurred on July 17, 1944, at the Port Chicago Naval Magazine in Port Chicago, California, United States. Munitions detonated while being loaded onto a cargo vessel bound for the Pacific Theater of Operations, killing 320 sailors and civilians and injuring 390 others.

Mindanao Island- An Island in the Philippines where the US Navy the and Army used the shore for Ammo and transportation means where the inland was controlled by the Japanese which led into a battle. The Battle of Mindanao was fought by United States forces and allied Filipino guerrillas against the Japanese from 10 March to 15 August 1945 on the island of Mindanao in the Philippines in a series of actions officially designated as Operation VICTOR V. It was part of the campaign to liberate the Philippines during World War II. The battle was waged to complete the recapture of the southernmost portions of the archipelago

Battle of Anzio- The Battle of Anzio was a battle of the Italian Campaign of World War II that took place from January 22, 1944 (beginning with the Allied amphibious landing known as Operation Shingle) to June 5, 1944 (ending with the capture of Rome). The operation was opposed by German forces in the area of Anzio and Nettuno.

Operation Fortitude- This was the code name for a World War II military deception employed by the Allied nations as part of an overall deception strategy (code named Bodyguard) during the build-up to the 1944 Normandy landings. Fortitude was divided into two sub-plans, North and South, with the aim of misleading the German high command as to the location of the invasion.

Operation Shingle- Operation Shingle is the name given to an amphibious landing by the Allies in Italy during World War II. It took place on January 22, 1944, under the command of United States Major General John P. Lucas. The object, which was successfully achieved, was to land sufficient forces to outflank the Germans along the Winter Line and set up an assault on Rome itself.

Operation Ten-Go- Operation Ten-Go was a Japanese naval operation plan in 1945, consisting of four likely scenarios. Its first scenario, Operation Heaven One became the last major Japanese naval operation in the Pacific Theater of World War II.

References

Material reference for the story...

- Lombardo Family War Letters
- The Official Chronology of the U.S. Navy in World War II https://www.ibiblio.org/hyperwar/USN/USN-Chron.html
- National Achieves online and in Washington DC: https://www.archives.gov/research/military/navy-ships
- Leon Grabowsky http://digital.lib.ecu.edu/11270
- Fifth Army at the Winter Line https://history.army.mil/books/wwii/winterline/winter-fm.htm
- WW2 Reference Wiki-Pedi https://en.wikipedia.org/wiki/World_War_II_casualties
- WW2 Last Letter https://www.washingtonpost.com/news/worldviews/wp/2014/06/05/a-u-s-soldiers-last-letter-home-before-he-died-on-d-day/?noredirect=on&utm_term=.dc824ac6819c
- US Navy Cook (A Hero) https://www.guns.com/news/2018/12/07/pearl-harbor-the-cook-who-took-up-a-machine-gun-and-put-it-to-good-use-photos

www.lettersforannie.com

Now on DVD

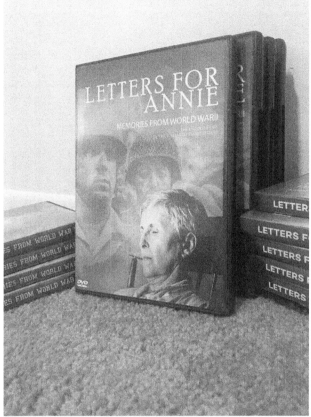

Learn more about the Lombardo Story.

Now on DVD at www.LettersForAnnie.com **or Stream the Film at** www.Vimeo.com/ondemand **and search for, "Letters for Annie."**

More information about the film at www.McGeeProductions.Us

Film Photos

Tommy Fury as Tony Lombardo

Ronnie White Jr as Captain Edwards

Brian Masters as PFC Jack Barnhart
Patrick McGee as Pat Lombardo

Christopher Silva as Lt. Commander Grabowsky

James Malcolm as Vic Lombardo

Amber Namery as Annie Connerton
Joe Wilkicki as John Lombardo

Logan Raposo as John Lombardo
Patrick McGee as Pat Lombardo

Mauricio Viteri as German Solider

About Joseph McGee

Joseph McGee is an American Author residing in Connecticut & New Jersey. He is a writer, director, and film producer of McGee Productions. Please follow my other work mentioned below:

- Leadership Lessons Inspired By a Six-Year Old
- The White House Is Fake
- Reflections: Project Chameleon (Coming 2020)

For more information follow me at www.jmcgeebooks.com or www.McGeeProductions.us

FOLLOW US AT
WWW.LETTERSFORANNIE.COM

54657184R00095

Made in the USA
Columbia, SC
03 April 2019